About the Author

It is safe to say Jerry Bradley has a degree in life! He has worked in a range of jobs: building racing cars, welding, bricklaying in Europe, market trading and as a locksmith.

In 2012, his wife of 29 years became ill and he became her full time carer. This was when he discovered a passion for writing. His wife, Irene, lost her battle with Dementia in 2015.

Jerry now lives in West Sussex and is the proud Dad of two daughters, Amanda & Hannah.

He does his best writing late at night and sometimes into the small hours but still finds time for martial arts, keep fit, golf and most of all, having fun!

www.jerrybradley.co.uk
Facebook: Jerry Bradley-Author

Acknowledgements

A huge thank you to Chris Day and the team at Filament. With a special thanks to Joan Grady who edited the Candy Man: she took this incredible story and sprinkled magic dust on it!

Dedication

This is dedicated to the four amazing people
who have helped me most in my life.

My late wife, Irene Joy Bradley, my late mum, Margaret, and
my daughter and son-in-law, Hannah & Peter Cohen.

Thank you.

In memory of my late wife, each book I sell myself I will make a
voluntary donation to Dementia UK.

From concrete jungle to king of the world
There is a price to be paid for everything.

THE CANDY MAN

THE HIGHS AND THE HIGHS

JERRY BRADLEY

Published by
Filament Publishing Ltd
16, Croydon Road, Waddon, Croydon,
Surrey, CR0 4PA, United Kingdom
Telephone +44 (0)20 8688 2598
Fax +44 (0)20 7183 7186
info@filamentpublishing.com
www.filamentpublishing.com

ISBN 978-1-912635-54-2.

Printed by IngramSpark

Contents

Chapter 1

I was six years old when I first met my grandpa at a hotel in London. He'd flown in from Southern Ireland, just to see me. What a nice old man. I was excited to meet him. I spent a couple of hours with him, supervised of course. He stood up as I entered the room and greeted me with open arms. He stepped back, put his hands up like a boxer ready to fight, a giant of a man.

He shared some pearls of wisdom: never back down from a fight, stand your ground. Be the very best, at whatever you do. Be bold, be brave, be a leader. He threw a few air punches, then he coughed and sat down.

I sat on his knee while we went through a box of photos. One showed him, boxing gear on, holding up a large belt. He told me it was a Lonsdale belt — he'd been the British heavyweight champion. One photo showed my mum. He told me the story about my mum and dad. How my dad had disappeared the day I was born. How my mum passed away soon afterwards. Then he said how sorry he was that he had to go away too. He was going to a place in heaven. He had no choice. I pondered, for just a moment, deep in thought.

"Grandpa," I said, "Did my dad have a choice?"

'Yes he did, son," he replied, with a sad look on his face. "He chose to run away.'

"Why did he run away Grandpa? Was dad scared of me?"

There was no answer.

Right then, I made up my mind. My dad was a coward. Only cowards run away. At that moment, I hated my dad. I raged inside. I vowed I'd never run away, from anything or anyone. I'd stand my ground. I'd never rest until I'd made my dream come true. I was going to rescue a beautiful princess, marry her and live in a big house on a mountain.

I shared my thoughts with Grandpa. He smiled, and said: "Go live your dream Jimmy. Go live your dream."

He gave me a little book called 'The Bible' as we were saying our goodbyes, as well as the box of photos, and a large, hardback book on martial arts. He said it had belonged to my mum. I thanked him, gave him a hug. I looked up at him, glanced at the woman from social services. Grandpa had tears in his old eyes as I went on my way.

I never saw him again. He passed away a couple of months later. I was on my own. I knew, even then, that I had to prepare for the journey ahead. As the social services woman drove me back home, I was deep in thought.

I went to my room and carefully put the Bible and my book in my drawer. Closing my eyes, thinking about Grandpa and my dream, I drifted away to a happy place. A place where mum was alive, and she and me and Grandpa lived in that house on the mountain.

Chapter 2

My mum came into my bedroom, smiling. "Happy birthday, James," she said, handing me a card. It was a Saturday afternoon and I was 8 years old. I put my martial arts book, my prized possession, down, thanked her for the card.

Really, life was okay. My adoptive parents weren't too bad. Creatures of habit, they liked to meet their friends at the local pub most evenings for a drink or two. He worked for the local council as a bin man. She was a housewife. Our two-bedroom, 6th floor flat was clean and tidy. It wasn't too bad. I still felt life could be a hell of a lot better.

What did I know? I was a messed-up kid, with a lot of anger running through me. Anger at being alone. At my dad, for leaving me. At my life, for being just 'okay'.

I rolled off the bed, put my old, worn-out trainers on. Then out to the stairway. I ran all the way down, then back up, two stairs at a time. It got my heart pumping, made me feel good. I did that four times, then glanced at my watch. Back to the flat. Twenty press-ups, twenty squats, twenty sit-ups. A quick shower and fresh, clean clothes. We had a sandwich as an early dinner. At 6 pm, on the dot, we all went to the pub.

I had to go too, because they couldn't afford a childminder. That's what they told me. I couldn't go inside. I sat outside and waited. Mum brought me out a can of fizzy drink and a bag of crisps. I wandered across the road to the local martial arts centre and watched the people training. I studied them, their moves. It was amazing. Karate, kickboxing, traditional boxing. I was so engrossed in watching, trying to copy the moves, I didn't notice it was raining. A tall old man, with an umbrella, appeared by my side. His voice startled me.

"What's your name, boy?" he asked.

"James Blake," I replied.

"Where are your parents?" I pointed to the boozer.

He nodded and said: "You best come inside, out of the rain."

I was soaked to the skin. Not a bad idea, I thought. So I followed him in.

The hall was buzzing, exciting, amazing. The man pointed to the changing room and said: "Go dry yourself off." I went in, found a towel, took my wet clothes off. With nothing else to do, I did twenty press-ups. At which point, a young guy walked in carrying a white karate uniform. I put it on. Even though it was huge on my small body, I felt like this was a magical place. It was a wonderful moment in my short life. I went back into the hall. The man shouted across to me, "James, stand at the back."

That's how my martial arts journey began. I was enrolled in the boxing and martial arts clubs, started training six evenings a week. Every week I tried to give the instructor — Bill — my two quid pocket money. Every week, he refused to take it. Which, to be honest, was fine by me. He was a good guy, for sure.

When training finished at five to ten, I'd change fast, head back across the road to wait for my parents to come out of the pub. We'd walk back to the flat, stopping for a takeaway along the way. They'd always start arguing.

Inside I'd go to my room, shut the door against their noise and open my special book, feeling lucky. I was learning. Bill was strict, he made us train hard. He was teaching us. Teaching us how to control the violence, how to switch it on and off in our minds. It was so easy for me. Like clicking my fingers. Or flicking a light switch. Bang: on. Bang: off. One moment happy, in a split second, darkness. Meeting violence with violence, learning how to survive in hostile surroundings. You get knocked down, you get back up. Strike hard and fast. No fear, no mercy. No emotion.

Chapter 3

The first time I saw my dad hit my mum, I was 9 years old. At first I froze, not sure what to do. Then I heard a voice in my head, shouting, "Attack! Attack!" I jumped in hard, throwing punch after punch. He just pushed me aside and kept going. I got up and weighed in again. I had to stop him. His back was to me, he was bent over my mum. I picked up a chair and smashed it down hard on his back with all my might. He slumped to the floor. "Don't hit my mum, you bastard!" I yelled.

I ran to my room, slammed the door, picked up my book. It was quiet. Next day, neither of them remembered a thing. They'd been far too pissed.

When I was 10 years old, a teacher at school wanted the class to draw a picture of our parents and our home. I looked at the blank piece of A4 paper, paused for a few seconds, then started drawing. I did my best. I thought it looked good. The teacher collected everything up, looked through them. Before I left the classroom that day, she asked me to stay behind.

She wanted me to explain my drawing. So I did. My mum was asleep, lying on the sofa, surrounded by flowers with angels watching over her. She looked so beautiful. On the other side of the drawing, my dad was on his knees, a sword sticking right through his chest. A fire was raging all around him. The teacher looked at me seriously and said, "James? Why have you drawn your dad like this?"

"Because he ran away from me miss," I said, quietly. "Ran away when I was a baby. Can I have my drawing, please?"

Still looking troubled, she handed it to me. I put it in my bag and went home. The drawing just expressed the mixed-up, burning emotions running through my head. My desire to punish the one who had deserted me. My feeling that life could have been so much better. All I had now was my book, my training and those little, violent voices in my head that helped when things got tough.

At 12 years old, one of the school bully boys thought he'd steal my bag. Three seconds later he was on the ground with a broken nose and two missing front teeth. He bawled his eyes out, his face was covered in blood. It was an important lesson for me. Now I knew my fighting skills worked in real life, not just knocking out my drunk dad, half way to unconsciousness already. I'd felt a powerful surge as I struck him down. It was all so easy.

No-one had liked that bully. They were scared of him. Now they were scared of me. I had no friends. Didn't care. Didn't want them. Didn't need them.

My first official Amateur Boxing Association bout was on my 14th birthday. As I stepped in the ring, I glanced over to my opponent. Smiled. He was in big, big trouble. I was so hungry. I couldn't wait to test my skills. I'd trained hard, but I'd only been sparring until this moment. This was the real deal. My coach told me how to get noticed — put on a good show for the crowd. I looked around. There were some fit birds in there, watching and waiting to see two young men slugging it out, to see blood. Did they get their kicks from this? It made me wonder. Who was I to judge?

The bell went. This was it. Nowhere to run, nowhere to hide. I was ready. Switch it on. I ducked his aggressive punches and went in hard, guns blazing. A quick combination — jab, jab, right uppercut, left hook — then a big right hook aimed at his temple. Fuck it, no show tonight. He hit the canvas hard, out for the count.

That became my pattern. I was a savage fighter, knocked out all my opponents. And I learned to entertain the crowd, beating them up first, then finishing them off. A noble art, boxing. So they told me. One day, people would be chanting my name.

However savage it might have been, it kept me out of trouble and off the streets. It made me a machine, all speed and power. When Bill died just after my first fight, the dojo/boxing clubs were taken over by a younger guy. He didn't do freebies. Now I had a monthly subscription to pay.

No chance of getting that from home. My parents had given in to booze. He'd lost his job. She'd lost the will to give a shit. The flat was a total mess. They were letting the side down, fucking everything up, drinking themselves into oblivion. Why? I was so mad at them. I had to keep training, keep learning, keep clawing my way out of this shit hole. So I went on the rob. I didn't have a choice.

Chapter 4

Susan arrived in my life on my 15th birthday. And what a present that was — the best gift a 15-year-old boy could wish for. Goodbye virginity, hello brilliant girlfriend.

Susan had shoulder length, dark brown hair. 5ft 6in, dark skin, athletic body, and a sexy smile. She was by far the hottest girl I'd ever met, as well as being good company. Not to mention great sex. We'd hook up every Sunday evening at the park, away from my pissed-up parents, who'd now progressed into drugs as well. They were both a fucking waste of space.

At 16 years old, I left school with no qualifications. I had alcoholic, drug-abusing parents, lived in a high rise block in a concrete jungle in the east end of London. Doing what I needed to survive, hungry as an old grizzly waiting for salmon to swim up his river. Trust me, there weren't too many options available.

So I was doing bad things. I had no choice. My parents no longer bought food. Spent what little they had on booze. I was eating out most of the time to get away from the squalor. Bailiffs at the door most weeks. Just the way it was. Susan helped me out, when she could, with cash or food. I had training fees to pay. Martial arts and boxing were my drug. They kept me sharp, focused. Cash had to come from somewhere.

I picked my targets with care. I watched and waited until they came out of a pub or club, drunk, then pushed them into an alleyway and mugged them. I didn't know any other way to stay alive. I'd tried to get work, failed. And I never got caught. I was careful. There are four ways to get caught: red-handed, grassed up, seen on CCTV or leave fingerprints. Those didn't happen to me. I stayed in quieter areas, no cops around. Knew where the cameras were. Wore gloves. And, at five-eight, built like a solid brick wall, hard as fuck and not to be messed with, no-one was going to grass.

Then I got a big break. I convinced an old trader at the local indoor market to give me a chance. His name was Geoff, a scruffy old geezer. The punters liked him. His tired old stall was my ticket out, my way to earn an honest living. The first few days flew by in a blur. As they turned into weeks and months, I learned the art of selling, had a bit of banter with the punters and, for the first time in my life, had some fun and laughter. I was earning. I was paying my way without stealing. I was training hard, eating well. Life was brilliant.

Come the end of September, trade was slow. Geoff normally closed up the stall, took himself and his good lady wife away to Spain for a bit of sun and some much-needed rest. An idea had started to form. An amazing, money-making plan. It was actually Susan who gave me the inspiration. She'd made me some homemade fudge, from an old recipe her Grandma had given her. It tasted great, so much better than the cheap, crappy stuff Geoff sold from the stall. So I'd become a retailer of high-quality, handmade sweets, fudge and chocolates. With a little something extra stashed inside.

Out of sight, out of mind. That's what I told myself. I'd be selling delicious, homely confectionery, I wasn't going to be some scum drug lord. Clean as a whistle. A good guy. A good guy making the vast amounts of money he needed to realise his dreams. A big house, big garden, maybe even an indoor pool. Loads of space for a wife and kids. A calm, peaceful life, out in the country. No violence, no drama, no stress. No need for those voices in my head.

I convinced Geoff to let me run the stall in his absence. Yep. Game on.

Chapter 5

I wasn't the only one on our manor watching to see who could be robbed. Stabbings and shootings were everyday events. I'd always kept my head down, tried not to get involved. Now I had a job, so I had money. I was a target. Fuck. I didn't need any trouble right now, not when I was about to start a whole new direction in life. That Saturday, after Geoff closed up and paid me in good old cash, I ran back to the flat to get changed for training. I grabbed my bag, headed out the door. Down, down the concrete stairs. I turned the corner with three flights still to go. Fuck. Two guys were waiting. I knew who they were and what gang they were in. I turned fast and ran back up to the nearest landing, ducked around the corner. They chased. Being a victim wasn't on my wish list.

They came steaming around the corner and saw me too late. Bang, bang, bang. The first guy went down in three strikes: nuts, knee and throat. I yanked the flick knife out of his hand and weighed in properly, slashing the other guy across the face three times and kicking him hard in the ribcage. He fell backwards, down the stairs. I looked at the first guy, still on the floor, and the knife in my hand. Then I stabbed him, again and again. I picked him up and threw him over the railings. Then I went after the other fool, finished him off, too. A few moments of madness and it was all done. They'd have murdered me for a couple of hundred quid. Fucking bastards, wasting my time and energy.

I looked up at the bloodbath on the stairwell. Stairway to hell. I ran back to the flat, took my blood-stained clothes off, cleaned myself up fast. Chucking the bloodied clothes in a bag, I went back out into the night. The main thing in my mind was not being late for training. I just made it on time.

Two hours later, after a good solid lesson, I jogged back to the flat. Lot of police cars about. There had been two deaths. I was suitably shocked, of course. Such terrible news, so close to home. Just another Saturday in this hellhole.

I got back home, such as it was. Pissed parents, crappy broken furniture — it looked more like a dirty squat than a home. I had my own life now. I used the place to shower and sleep. I washed my clothes at the local launderette. I'd saved a lot of my wages and had a small stash of cash hidden away. Now was the time to raise the stakes. I quietly went to my room, got out my well-hidden cash. Then back out into the darkness.

I knew a lot of people in the manor. If you had cash, you could buy anything. I went to the local pub. Not the one my parents frequented. Not one many people frequented. Not people you'd like to hang out with, anyway.

I saw the guy I was searching for, walked up to him and asked for a word. He nodded, turned and walked out. I followed him. Now it was a private business meeting, exactly as I wanted. I told him what I was after. He burst out laughing. "What a fucking prick," I thought. "Why do I bother with fools? He's not a businessman. In his eyes, I'm just a kid. He only sees what he wants to see, here's what he wants to hear." I sighed, shook my head and punched him hard. My fist crunched into his unprotected rib cage. He stopped laughing then. Went down on his knees, gasping for much-needed breath.

"I have the cash," I said. "I'll drop by tomorrow at seven to collect my goods. Oh, and do take me seriously. I have a plan. A chance for us both to make easy money."

I turned and walked out of the bleak, barely-lit pub alleyway, jogged back to my so-called home. Went to my room, closed the door, sat on the bed. I closed my eyes, dozed into a deep sleep, with my book safely by my side.

●

Chapter 6

I needed Susan's culinary skills to finalise my plan. I had to move fast, get a trial run going while Geoff was in Spain. Susan had to teach me how to make the fudge just like her Grandma. My one day off was Monday. I got up early, spent all morning cleaning the kitchen, to make it presentable for when Susan arrived. Gave the useless parents £50 to fuck off out and get drunk, away from me for a few hours. I couldn't stand either of them. Piss-heads, wasters, scumbags. Just being in the same room was a challenge. If only I'd been adopted by anyone else.

Susan turned up, 2 pm on the dot. She'd brought everything we needed. She wrapped her slender arms around my neck, kissed me, and gave me a card and a gift. I'd forgotten it was my 17th birthday. My mind was on business. Susan had bought me a white shirt so I'd look smart on the stall. Such a kind gesture. She was so brilliant. This was going to be a doddle.

We had fun working together. After we made our first tray of amazing fudge, I tried my shirt on. It fitted perfectly. I hoped it made me look older, smarter, more like the businessman I wanted to be. I felt good. I thanked Susan, and we kissed. Then my adoptive parents came crashing back early, destroyed my happy bubble. Pissed up, arguing as usual. This was so embarrassing. I was fucking fuming.

We packed up all the stuff and legged it. Susan took it all in her stride. I apologized to her. She looked at me. "I'm not in love with your parents," she said. "I'm in love with you." I was a bit taken aback, but I smiled. The future could be good, with Susan by my side. The love thing? Hold the horses, girl, slow down. I wasn't sure if I could love anyone. Love was for fools.

"Let's walk back to yours," I said. "Via the park." Smiling, she agreed. We found a quiet spot for a quickie, her pinned up against a tree, dress around her slim waist. Just two teenagers having fun. Then a slow walk to her home. I kissed her goodnight and watched her cross the road, making sure she was safe inside before turning away. All sorted. I put my hood up, then headed off to collect my package. I entered the pub, bang on time. I should have been tooled up and on red alert. My mind was miles away, on Susan, her smooth skin and hot, inviting pussy. I never saw the bat.

Whoosh, thud, right on the side of my mixed up head. It dropped me like a sack of spuds. Half conscious, I was dragged into the dark alleyway. They kicked the shit out of me. All I'd wanted was to buy some fucking drugs and make some fucking money. A simple transaction. Now my new white shirt was ruined. Happy birthday, me.

I'd pissed the drug dealer off. Error of judgment. He, on the other hand, had made a huge mistake. He didn't know what I was capable of. Should have done his homework. He fucked up. He should have killed me.

The goons went back into the busy pub. I laid still until I heard the door click shut. I moved my hand to my pocket and touched the roll of banknotes. I got up, wiped the blood off my face. Took a deep breath. No broken bones. Good. I was ready for battle. No mercy. Time to use my skills.

I walked back into the pub. A quick look round. Not too bad. Five of them. Ladies and gentlemen, place your bets. I walked to the bar. The pretty barmaid stared at me, shock and fear in her sparkling eyes. "Two bottles of lager please," I said. "Leave the tops on." She placed two bottles on the bar and backed away. I handed her twenty quid and said, "Keep the change."

The pub fell silent. All eyes were on me. My targets were by the main door. Three on the bench, two on chairs, backs towards me. The big guy stood up and started towards me, baseball bat in hand. So I knew who hit me. I smiled and nodded. He stopped two paces away from me, said, "Look, kid, best fuck off or you're gonna get hurt." Blah, blah, blah, don't be fucking stupid, blah, blah. He pointed to the exit. I moved in.

One hard kick to his left knee, a loud crunch. As he started to buckle, I shoved the beer bottles, cap end first, into his eyes, then smashed and twisted both against his ugly face, ripping his flesh open. A split second before he fell, a hard straight-finger strike to his unguarded throat. He'd let go of the bat, trying to hold his broken knee. His face was covered in blood. He was trying to scream. Two swift punches to his head, one to the side of his jaw and one upwards to his nose.

I caught the bat before it hit the floor and charged in on my enemies.

I hit the first guy with the bat, split his head like a coconut. A full-throttle sidekick later, his pal was out for the count too. Holding the bat like a spear, I smashed it into the other guy's face: bang, bang, bang — blood was flowing tonight. He fell forward, didn't move.

The drug dealer had reached into his jacket and drawn a gun. I didn't even blink. I knocked the gun out of his hand with the bat as he was standing up, then delivered a hard kick to his groin. Spinning into a spectacular roundhouse kick, I broke his jaw, then pulled him away from the table. Two punches to his ribcage, right on the spot, in front of his heart and he fell over, laying on his side. Dead.

I went through his pockets, found a wad of notes. I picked up the gun and looked around. What a fucking mess. Most of the punters had legged it. To the few who'd stayed to watch the show, I yelled, "When the old bill come, you never saw me, right? Don't make me come back in here and get Biblical!" I looked at their faces. Not likely anyone of them would be blabbing. Just to press it home, I pointed the gun at the big guy and squeezed the trigger. Fired until the gun was empty, twelve bullets. I looked around the silent room and said, quietly, "Don't fuck with me. Don't ever fuck with me."

I walked out into the darkness. My heart was beating, adrenaline pumping, mind racing. I'd never felt anything like this before. I had to calm down. I had to dump the bat and gun. I had to get cleaned up. I had to find a new dealer. And all the time I kept singing, in my head: "Happy birthday to me, happy birthday to me..." I was 17, for fuck's sake. I should be out, having fun, not obliterating drug dealers in shitty backstreet pubs. I gently jogged home.

The dead dealer's wedge of cash lifted my mood. Not bad. A couple of grand. I went to the bathroom, undressed, wrapped a clean hand towel around my head and showered. The wound on my head, had stopped bleeding, so I just needed to clean it and bandage it up. I put fresh clothes on, then headed to the local 24-hour shop. Couldn't go to the hospital, too many questions. I needed wipes, gauze and some bandages. Simple. I had a £20 note on me and a towel around my head, and I was still in a bad mood. Just as I went to the counter to pay, the auto door opened. For fuck's sake, not tonight.

In walks some dick with a knife in his hand. He shouts at the cashier to give him the takings. Not my problem. He'd only get a few hundred quid. I watched the cashier empty both tills and put the cash in a bag. Then the guy looks at me. "Give me the note," he said. I shook my head wearily, and spoke quietly. "Look, pal, as you can see, I'm having a bad hair day. I need this money," I said. Being a good guy. Giving him a choice. He didn't take it. "Give me the note," he said again. "Give me it, or I'll cut you up."

What a birthday. Not even a cake with candles. I ignored the idiot, put the stuff on the counter and gave the £20 note to the surprised cashier. The guy with the knife moved in. I grabbed his knife hand, twisted his wrist, punched him hard on his chin, then hit him with an elbow strike to the nose. I wrenched the knife out of his grasp. I dragged him outside, out of sight and slit his throat. Then went back in the shop and said: "Get this mess cleaned up, keep your mouth shut and wipe the CCTV recording."

The stunned cashier nodded. He knew me. Lived in the same block. Took me back to the camera desk, where I watched him wipe the drive. I handed him the bag of stolen cash, picked up my stuff and said: "Keep the change." As I left he was dragging a mop and bucket over to the pool of blood on the floor.

I dumped the cleaned-off knife in a skip on my way back, shaking my head over yet another set of bloodied clothes. I'd buy some more tomorrow. A birthday treat.

Chapter 7

I got back to my so-called home. What a fucking shit-hole. My adoptive parents were in. I heard them call out. "Happy birthday, James!" This was incredible. They must have seen my birthday card from Susan. "Just going to the loo," I called back.

I cleaned and bandaged my head the best I could, put on a baseball cap, changed into clean clothes and added the clothes to the bag containing the others. For one wild, delusional moment, I thought my parents might have got me a card or a present. But no. They wanted me — me — to take them out for drinks. Talk about taking the piss. They sat me down and told me a story. Maybe they thought in their fucked-up heads that telling me the truth would soften me up, make me give them more money. They both stunk of booze.

I listened. I'd been adopted as a baby. I already knew that. What I didn't know was that I had siblings. A sister and a brother. Originally, they'd taken us all in. But they just couldn't cope with two young kids and a baby. So my family was split up. Why had no one ever told me this? Why hadn't social services mentioned it? Why my grandpa? Maybe he thought it was best not to, he was a wise old man.

It wasn't a story I'd expected on my special day. I went to my bedroom, got out my stash of cash, gave them £60. They went out to get drunk. I was breathing fire. I sat in silence and digested the information. Rage took control. I hated them. Bastards. Couldn't cope, split my family up. Why'd they bothered keeping me? Why had the powers that be not kept the three of us together? Cold hatred ran through my body. The voices started up, screaming for retribution. I clicked my fingers. On, off. On, off.

I went back to my bedroom. Put my book and all my cash in a bag. Then I waited. Fucking bastards, my so-called parents. Both a total waste of space.

If you aren't happy with your life, you have to change it. That was my plan right now, to change my life, to change it fast. I closed my eyes and looked into the future. Dream big, make it happen. It was a cool house. Long sweeping driveway, large landscaped garden. Top of the range motor parked outside. Up four solid stone steps to a big oak front door, into a hallway with an Italian marble floor and a grand spiral staircase. The huge crystal chandelier came to life, as I switched the lights on. Two beautiful children running down the stairs to greet me. A wonderful wife — not Susan. "Hello James," she said. "How was your day? Supper will be ready soon."

A happy home, filled with love and laughter. With a family. I was a lucky guy.

The dream faded as I opened my eyes. After spending all the cash I'd given them for booze, my unreal parents were home, both drunk and carrying a bag each. They came into the lounge, put their bottles of cheap crappy cider on the coffee table, sat down. I watched as they drank the lot. It was like a horror movie, a fucking nightmare. They didn't even thank me. My dad tried to light a fag from his Zippo. Passed out before he could manage it. Mum was also unconscious on the badly-stained, threadbare sofa. I shook my head, stood up. I couldn't live here anymore. Tonight, bridges were going to burn.

I stood behind my adoptive mum, put my hands on her head, twisted with all my might, heard the snap. I pushed my dad off the chair. Disgusting, he'd pissed himself. I put two towels over his face, I wasn't going to get covered in blood again. I rained down punch after punch until he was dead, face smashed in good and proper. If you do a job, do it right, right? Going into the small kitchen, I turned on all the gas rings without lighting them. Paused for a moment then, with my bare hands, ripped the old cooker away from the wall completely. Gas hissed out.

I picked up the yellow tin of lighter fuel and went back into the lounge. I picked up the Zippo, flicked it into life, stared at the hypnotic flame. I squeezed the lighter fuel over the chair and the sofa, chucked some old newspapers on the floor. Dropping the empty tin, I looked at the flame of revenge and let go. I stepped back, picked up my bag and left the shit hole for the last time. I didn't look back.

A fresh start now. I started walking to find a secure hiding place for my bag. 300 yards away from the flats, I turned and waited. There was an almighty explosion. I smiled, walked on to the local graveyard. Pushing a heavy, flat stone away from its resting place, I dumped my bag inside the hole and pushed the stone back. Then I sat on the moss-covered stone and waited an hour.

I checked my old but trusty digital watch. Time to make my way back. As I turned the corner, it looked like a scene from a disaster movie. Fire engines, ambulances, police cars. I'd heard the sirens. The area had been cordoned off. People scattered around, some with grey blankets over their shoulders, people on stretchers. It was total chaos. The crappy concrete block had been evacuated. I ran up to the police cordoned off area, clearly hysterical. "What's happened here?" I yelled. "What's happened? I live here!"

The copper escorted me to the emergency command area, where a tent had been erected. I was asked to sit down and answer some questions. My name, what flat I lived in. The woman listened to me sadly. 'I'm sorry to tell you the bad news," she said. "We believe the explosion was from your flat. We also believe both your parents were killed in the blast, we can't officially identify the bodies. The explosion was too severe."

I put my face in my hands and started shaking, obviously in shock. I was taken to a B&B for the night, a social services official by my side. All I had were the clothes I was wearing. "Don't worry, James," she said. "I'll be here at 10 am tomorrow, then we can get you all the things you need." I thanked her, this older woman. Mid-fifties, grey untidy hair, 5ft 4in, way overweight. Kind. A new experience for me.

For tonight, I had a new place to sleep. It was clean and tidy. Tomorrow, I'd be given new clothes for free. I'd literally blown away my past. Now I could concentrate on business, on making the vast amounts of money that would make my dream home a reality. The world was my oyster. I felt brilliant. At peace. The voices, finally, were silent.

I sat on the bed and looked around my new home. It ticked all the boxes. Good location, paid for by the council. I reached in my jacket pocket, got my phone out and turned it on. It rang almost at once. Susan must have been out of her mind with worry. Her voice was close to hysterical. I managed to calm her down, told her I was OK. She'd seen the news on TV. Headline news, council tower block evacuated after massive blast. Some speculation about terrorism, other reports about an apparent gas explosion. The Old Bill weren't sure about the number of fatalities. Early stages of investigations. Body count believed to be 18 dead, loads more badly injured. She wasted an hour of my life, twittering on. Drama, fucking drama.

Then Geoff called, also making sure I was alive. Told me to take all the time off I needed. Not my plan. I told him I wanted to keep busy, I wanted still to run the stall while he was away. "Whatever you need, James," he said. "Whatever you need."

Thank fuck for that.

•

Chapter 8

I'd come to realise something. I wasn't going to marry Susan. She hadn't been in my dream. Her concern and sympathy over the explosion dragged across my nerves instead of soothing me. She'd been good to me, a great friend as well as a girlfriend. I owed her something. So I called her that night, after an amazing fish and chip supper supplied by the B&B owners, intending to let her down gently.

Before I could start, she did. To my astonishment, it turned out she was supposed to be marrying someone else on her 18th birthday. A marriage arranged by her parents. Bit of a relief for me. Except that she didn't want to do it. She wanted to tie the knot with me.

She sobbed her heart out as she unravelled her story. I reassured her, told her I'd sort it out. I had a lot on my plate right now. Two funerals to arrange, fudge to make, stock to buy, stall to set up. The state would step in until I was 18, so at least I didn't have to think about finding somewhere to live. I had a few days, just a few days, to prepare and run the stall my way. Still, it was late and I'd had a busy day. I'd crack on with my tasks tomorrow.

I opened my window, quietly climbed out and jogged to the graveyard. I retrieved my bag and ran gently back to the B&B. I had my book and my cash. Didn't need anything else. I was young, free, alive, positive and full of energy. I lay down, closed my eyes. The bed was so comfortable. I was floating on a cloud. I drifted off and slept soundly till morning.

When I got up, I used the power shower to wash away the past, put a clean dressing on my head, donned my cap and went downstairs. The television was blaring over a full English breakfast, the BBC news telling the story about the blast at the block.

The concrete 1960s shit hole would have to be demolished. Great news, I'd done them all a favour. They'd be rehoused. The other story was about an apparent gangland drug war — my battle at the pub. I must have put on a good show, because no-one had grassed me up. Both stories were front-page tabloid news. I should get a commission. It was my story. Robbing bastards, the press.

The doorbell rang. It was the social services woman. She came in, trilling to anyone who was listening, "Good morning, how are we all feeling today?" Stupid question. Although I'd had a good night's sleep and an excellent home-cooked breakfast, so I was feeling fantastic. The woman asked me to follow her to the sitting room, where she spoke swiftly and straight to the point.

I'd be placed in a youth home until the age of 18. Excellent, a roof over my head and decent food. The state would take care of the funeral arrangements. Even better. Because I was intending to contribute fuck all to them. I interrupted her flow of information to ask about my family. Could she help me track them down? She said they'd misplaced my details, and were trying to find my case folder. I asked her why I hadn't been told I had a family. She got flustered and brushed my question aside with something about bereavement counselling. I managed to keep a straight face. An hour later, in Marks & Spencer's, I was fully kitted out, loaded up with new clothes, shoes, underwear. Then a sports shop for trainers, tracksuits, t-shirts, sweatshirts, socks, the works. I felt like a new person.

Three days after that, I was on my way to my new home. We pulled up outside an old Victorian house with an amazing garden. I was introduced to the couple who ran the place, shown my room, told I could come and go as I pleased if I followed the rules. No alcohol, no drugs. No problem. I'd had enough of both to last a lifetime. Paperwork sorted, I thanked the social services lady for her help and sent her on her way. My new room, with en-suite shower, felt like a posh hotel. Home sweet home.

The following Tuesday, at 5.30am, I started my business. I'd put the word out on the street. By Wednesday, I was flat out busy. My supplier — no problems securing one this time — was a happy guy. I had a brilliant week. Sunday, after work, I jogged to the park to meet Susan. She was upset, crying. It was time to sort things out.

Then she dropped a fucking bombshell. She was pregnant and wanted to marry me, not this other guy, this arranged marriage guy. She quizzed me about my head wound and bruises. I told her I'd got mugged. She started crying again. Didn't know what to do. Fuck's sake.

A baby. We were still kids ourselves. What a fucking mess. All that time carefully using condoms. Fuck, fuck. In my mind, we only had one option — abortion. I had the cash, could set it up for her, get her the best of care. I sat with her for ages, neither of us saying much. My head, to be honest, was more full of plans for my own future. I only had one more week running the stall. I needed to find new premises, fast. This was not good. The week shot by.

Friday evening, jogging back from training, I stopped to tie the lace on my trainer. I stood up, then saw a woman exit a building, with two men either side of her. They were heading towards a parked car, with the back door open. Then another car screeched into the street. I stared in disbelief as two guys, with what looked like sub-machine guns in their hands, leaned out of the windows, ready to shoot up the street.

The guns weren't pointed at me. They were aimed at the woman. Not my fight or my problem — I wasn't a hero. But fuck it. Instinct kicked in and I dived towards the woman, bringing her to the ground. The whole scene went to slow motion. I used my body to shield her from harm. Crazy. The guns roared into life. Luckily, we'd hit the open car door and closed it before falling beside the car. Without a doubt that saved our lives.

The deafening roar of the guns went on. Two of her men were down, riddled with bullets. The other two were shooting back. Then the shooters' car raced off. Just another real-life drive-by shooting like you see in the movies, no big deal. Fucking mental. I breathed a deep, deep sigh of relief. My ears were ringing. I looked up. The driver of their car was dead, half his head splattered on the dashboard. No need to check his pulse. I glanced at the woman, she had fire in her eyes. She was pretty hot. I helped her up, asking, "Are you okay?" Kind of a silly question, what do you say in these situations?

She didn't answer. Instead, she took my hand and we ran to the nearest underground station entrance. Her two guys followed behind. She dialled her phone, spoke quickly in a foreign language. Signalled to me to wait. So we waited. Ten minutes later, three cars pulled up. We got in the middle one. Cool as a cucumber, she turned to me. "We'll drop you home," she said, quietly. Not a sign of shock.

I wanted to run. These were fucking crazy people. She was super attractive, so I went with the flow, told them my address. She held out her hand, saying, "You can call me Ling."

"James," I said, shaking her hand. Cool and dry. You'd have thought she'd just been for a business lunch.

As we pulled up outside the home, she said, "We'll see you tomorrow, 8am. Oh, sorry, my manners — thank you for saving my life. You are a brave man." The convoy drove off, into the night. What had I got myself into now? Life promised to be full of interest, at least, but did I need it? No, I fucking did not.

The morning after the shooting incident, as instructed, I was collected at 8am. A black Merc pulled up, I got in and we headed off. It quickly became apparent that we were going to Chinatown. Ling explained that she was taking me to meet her father. Turns out, the old boy couldn't do enough for me. I was a hero. I'd saved his precious daughter's life. He owed me, big time. Then he said words that were music to my ears, "Your actions have shown you are a brave and courageous man. If there is anything I can do to repay you, you have only to ask."

Carpe diem time. I was a 17-year-old kid with a big dream. I was going to grab this golden opportunity with both hands. If I went to the high street banks or Dragons' Den with my idea, they'd tell me politely to fuck off or, more likely, hold me in a room while they called the cops. I needed help to expand my business. This was life-changing stuff. I told him my plan. Three times, I had to explain it. Then we sat in silence, for a few minutes. Finally, he spoke. "Okay."

●

Chapter 9

The deal was done. It was perfect timing. I knew my plan worked. I'd open the stall for one last day, then I'd be free. With the Chinese backing me, I'd get premises, and a regular supply of top-quality drugs. We'd do a 50/50 split of the proceeds. I was safe and untouchable. I knew who they were. They all had a dragon tattoo on their necks. They were the feared Dragon Triad gang, and Ling's dad was the boss. I smiled and shook his hand.

After the meeting, I was driven to the market, my special fudge ready to sell. I'd made it myself, at the home. My two bodyguards stayed in the shadows.

Geoff had arrived back from Spain, and appeared at the stall that morning. The Chinese boss told me to concentrate on the shop and forget the crappy stall. I owed Geoff, so I did him a favour and bought him out so he could retire to Spain for good. I'd paid him back. Deal complete. Karma sorted. The stall was closed, forever. I was driven to my training session. My driver, the Merc and two minders would wait, then take me back to the youth home. I would have preferred to jog back, on my own, this wasn't the time to get picky.

Sunday morning. I was picked up again and taken back to Chinatown. I sat in the back of the Merc, one guy either side. Ling sat up front. We stopped outside a shop. "Will this do?" said Ling. "Yes," I said. "This will do nicely." I gave her the list of things I needed. She glanced down it, looked at me, smiled and said in her fluent, sharply-accented English, "We open a week tomorrow."

I was in business. We'd offer a free delivery service, cater for everyone. Stock only the best sweets and chocolates at rock bottom prices and the amazing, magical fudge. A smoke screen for the small packets of drugs put in the fudge before it set. The different flavour fudges were a code for different drugs. Simple. What could go wrong?

We'd also make the fudge, on its own, drug-free. I knew it would sell fast. Everything would be boxed up and sold in our designer boxes featuring my new logo: The Candy Man. It had a good ring to it. I was the Candy Man.

There was a lot for Ling's men to organize. For a start, the space at the back of the shop had be transformed into a kitchen. Could they pull it off in a week? With nothing else to do, I spent the next several days training hard. I had to keep busy. The following Sunday, I was back at the shop. As promised, without any hitch or drama, it was kitted out, fully stocked and ready to open. I was blown away. It looked fantastic. A fully-fitted kitchen, stainless steel worktops, all up to spec for hygiene regulations. The window display looked great. The designer boxes looked cool.

Ling watched as I showed two young Chinese women how to make the fudge and insert the small packets of cocaine or heroin before it set. Then she handed me a smart phone displaying our brand new, fully-functional website. Most of our initial business would be online. The products were coded, then packed and delivered, cash on delivery. Done.

I stood back and admired it all. No Susan this Sunday night, I was busy getting ready for business. I felt proud. This was our brand, our product. It was perfect. High season and time for the tourists to party, as well as our standard revelling customers. We'd taken drug dealing to the next level. It was like an express train screaming along the track to wealth and success. Nothing was going to stop me now.

The first day we took over £3,000. I closed the door bang on 6 pm, counted the cash, put it in two piles. Ling put one in a small holdall, nodded her pretty head and went on her way. I took the other to add to my stash. As the weeks shot by, business was brisk. I was calm and relaxed, no need for those voices in my head. I kept training, six evenings a week, was in great shape. Life was so good.

Three weeks later, I sat with the boss man, we had a meal, chatted about business. Ling was with us. He was powerful, evil. No doubt about it, I was in deep, shark-infested water up to my neck. It was working for me. We spoke briefly about the location of our next shop. We had to move fast, not waste time. We knew it worked, so it was green light all the way, go, go, go. The next day, Ling and I would start looking for new premises. All financed by the gang. "When will you be 18?" asked the boss man. I told him the date. "OK," he said. "You come and see me."

That evening, after training, I decided to jog back home. I cut through the park to lose my driver and two minders, who were following me in the Merc. I turned the corner and stopped, sharpish. Three guys stood in my way. "What's in the rucksack?" one of them asked. A gun in his right hand glistened in the moonlight. The guys were clearly of Chinese origin. The gun guy had a snake tattoo on the side of his neck. This was not a standard mugging.

My half of the shop takings were in my bag, plus my martial arts book. I'd dropped myself right in it. Clearly, I'd been watched. I knew I was fast, but fast enough to dodge bullets? Probably not.

Nevertheless, I had no time for bullshit. "Training gear," I said. "Although it's fuck all to do with you." Keep talking, keep talking, buy time to even the odds. A glint on his left hand caught my eye.

"Oh, by the way, your wife sucked my cock last night," I added. "Then I turned her over and fucked her up the arse. She squealed like a little pig. Loved having a big hard cock inside her."

I certainly had his full attention. He moved in close, raised the gun above his head, ready to strike. I stared into his eyes. He stared right back and saw death. Two shots rang out, and his two sidekicks were dead behind him. As his gun came down towards my head, I blocked his strike, then threw a spear hand blow to his throat. A swift hard kick to his groin followed by a right uppercut to his chin. He fell. I twisted the gun out of his hand and dropped it to the path. I pulled out my flick knife and stabbed him in both eyes. He was still conscious when I sliced both ears off. Blood on my hands again. He was screaming so loud by this time, I had no other choice — I slit his throat. I stepped back, turned and said: "What took you so long?" My two bodyguards had shot the other two guys. I was angry. Covered in blood. Again. I took it out on the two dead guys, out came their eyes and off came their ears. I glanced at my two minders. "Got a towel?" I asked.

We walked back to the Merc. One of my guys said, "Why did you cut their ears off and stab their eyes out?"

"So they won't see or hear what's coming in hell," I replied.

Six weeks after the explosion, my adoptive parents' funerals came and went. The nice couple who ran the youth home came with me. A scattering of old neighbors and some former drinking buddies were there too. Geoff and his wife Vera, to my surprise, turned up to support me in my time of grief. Ling and my minders sat by my side in the crematorium. Susan wasn't there.

<hr>

Chapter 10

A week later, I was in a small office at the adoption agency. An appointment had been arranged by the social services woman — they'd found my case notes. The woman behind the desk said, "This is how the system works. We'll contact both parties and see if we can arrange a meeting."

Blah, blah, blah. Rage filled me as she droned on. This was my family she was talking about. Where the fuck was her shitty system when I was 14 years old and needed help and food? Where was it when my family was being broken up? I asked her why we couldn't have stayed together. "At the time, we had no other choice," she said, and went straight back into her prepared script.

"If the parties do agree to have contact, we can start the ball rolling," she eventually finished. Yeah, right. I wasn't about to sit and wait any longer. I reached for my half-full glass of water and clumsily knocked it over. "Oops, sorry!" "Don't worry," she said, getting up with surprising speed. "I'll fetch some kitchen roll."

She left the room. I grabbed the paperwork, neatly stacked on her desk. There were the names I needed. Lisa Clarke and Robert Jones. My brother and my sister. Lisa was 2 years older than me, Robert was 3 years older. For fuck's sake. My sister had tried to have contact with me. It was all on record. Jesus Christ.

There was just one question left to answer. It burned inside me, tore me up every day. Why had my dad abandoned us? There were no excuses for his cowardice, not in my mind. One day I'd hunt him down and fucking murder him for what he'd put us through. Dirty, stinking bastard. I sat back down, filled with fury. The woman came back. I swallowed it down, helped her clean up the water. Of course, my brother and sister would want to meet me. It was a start. "Let's get started, please," I said. "Let's see if they agree to meet."

The shop was busy. I'd been at the right place, at the right time. Ling was like a shadow, watching my every move like a hawk. She was 22 years old, always immaculately dressed. Very attractive. She was one hot woman. And we got on well. Sadly, there was a giant, neon 'off-limits' sign over her head. Daughter of the boss. Entry forbidden. Meanwhile, it was a couple of weeks before Susan's 18th birthday, and her stupidly-arranged marriage. We'd been seeing less and less of each other. I didn't even know what she'd intended to do about the baby. This was the perfect time to expand our business, so I had enough to focus on.

We opened the shop, Ling by my side as usual. Trade was already brisk. Together, we packed the online orders, ready for delivery. Our drivers loaded up and went on their way. At lunchtime I decided to sort things with Susan. It was a week before her birthday. I called her and arranged to meet for dinner.

Ling's dad had done me a big favour. His network spanned the globe. He'd organised a place for Susan at a university in California. I was all set to be the good guy, to give her a better life. I'd already told her about it. She was, of course, excited, but tearful. She knew it was goodbye. We arranged to meet at 8pm that night. I had a gold bracelet to give her as a birthday gift, and a large envelope filled with cash, tickets to the States and a year's lease on an apartment near the university. I was a good guy.

It was like a farewell meal, a celebration of the good times. After dinner, we went to a nearby bar to meet Ling, her dad, and her brother Zen. My business partners. Susan went off to powder her nose. (Why do women say that? Why not just say 'I'm going for a piss'?) Ling leaned over and whispered in my ear, "If you fuck her, I'll cut your balls off."

I turned and stared. What? Was the off-limits boss's daughter actually coming on to me? I'd speak to her about it tomorrow. Tonight, I had to take Susan home. The Merc was a bit crowded, with my two bodyguards, me and Susan, when we arrived I walked with her to the front door, gently kissed her goodnight. "Don't you want to come in?" she asked, then giggled. "Come inside of me?" she added. She stank of booze. A real turnoff.

Not like her at all. She'd drunk a lot, also not like her. I wanted us to part friends, so I kissed her softly again, shaking my head. And realising I'd rather kiss crazy Ling. Enter the dragon zone at my peril. You only live once.

"When do you leave?" I asked. "Tomorrow," she said. "Tomorrow morning. A new life. Away from my parents. Away from all of it. Thank God. And thank you, James." Tears were welling. Nope, time to go. I gave her the envelope. Tickets, visas, lease agreements, £10k in cash. "Good luck girl," I whispered. "Go live your dreams." And I turned and walked out of her life. One less problem.

As I got back in the car, Ling's words played in my mind. Bollocks. One more item on the agenda. Fuck it, I'd deal with it later. My train of thought was interrupted by my driver. "We go meet boss," he said. Like I had a choice. We headed to Ling's dad's restaurant. I went in and was taken through to the kitchen and down the steep, narrow steps to the cellar.

Ling stood by her Dad, her brother the other side. Two guys were chained to a concrete post, gagged. Six other Triad members were also present. All eyes were on me, as the boss spoke. "These fools, they steal from us," he said. "I feel ashamed. You choose. Choose if they live or die."

They were two of our delivery men. Why would they steal from us? Didn't they know who we were? Did they have some kind of death wish? Staring at Ling's dad across the table, I realised this was a stern test. They wanted to see how far I'd go to protect our business. To exact the discipline needed in this kind of organisation. No problem.

An array of deadly weapons was laid out neatly on the table. Fuck, this could get messy. Yet more blood. No thanks. I picked up a silver handgun. It felt reassuringly good in my hand. "Got any cling film?" I asked. I got some blank looks in reply. Someone was sent to get some. "Wrap it round their heads," I said, when he returned. When he'd finished, I flicked back the safety catch and pointed the gun at the first guy's head. Squeezed three times. Turned to the other guy. Repeat. Excellent. It had worked. No spatter — the cling film kept it all in. Wiping the gun with a cloth, I put it neatly back on the table.

So noisy, I thought. Ears ringing. I should just have beaten them to death. Lesson learned: never fire a gun in a confined space.

I'd passed the test. Time to go home.

I was just settling down to sleep when there was a knock at the door. It was Janet, a new 'friend' from the home. We'd had an arrangement for a couple of months. She'd found me one night, making fudge in the kitchen, and we struck a little deal. She sucked my cock, and I paid her in drugs. I heard the door open, and Janet come in. She quietly closed the door, and smiled, dropping her bathrobe to the floor. Naked in the moonlight, she glowed. I sat up, swinging my legs over the edge of the bed. She knelt in front of me, sliding her warm, soft lips over my hardness, taking it deep into her mouth.

Her tongue worked wonders, flicking and licking, tickling and teasing. The woman knew how to give a blow job. I shot right down her throat. She simply stood up, wiped her mouth and held out her small left hand. I gave her a slab of fudge, complete with cocaine, for services rendered.

It wasn't a classy arrangement, but it worked for everyone and helped to pass the lonely evenings. We were both teenagers, inquisitive, experimenting, trying out new things. One night, we'd sneaked out of the home and gone to the local graveyard. I wanted to try something new. I'd visited a sex shop, on my way home, bought a new toy to try out. I showed it to Janet. A leather flogger. I'd been assured it wouldn't leave permanent marks or scars. Taking my clothes off, I braced my hands against a headstone, my back towards her. "Do it," I said. "Don't stop till I tell you. Do it hard enough, I'll give you a bonus."

The girl had some strength, she had to stop twice for a breather. We stopped after half an hour, I dressed and we went home. Janet got her special fudge, plus £200 in cash. I shut my door, undressed, looked in the mirror at her handiwork. I was marked. She'd beaten me alright. I'd felt nothing. No pain. At that moment, I knew no-one could ever hurt me.

Chapter 11

After Janet left, I lay back, mind racing. I'd never be able to sleep after this night's events. So when there was a knock at the window, it was almost a relief. I pulled back the curtain. Ling. Black hair shining in the moonlight. Looking nervous, on edge. What the fuck was going on tonight? Had I suddenly turned into some raging, irresistible stud? "I shouldn't be here," Ling whispered, climbing in the low window. "I like you. And there are things you need to know. Secrets. Secrets that must stay with us -" Her phone beeped suddenly, cutting her off.

A brief stream of Chinese whispers later, she turned back to me. "I have to go," she said, stepping closer. "We'll talk soon." Her sweet lips brushed mine, and she was back out the window and gone. Next second, my phone lit up. A text from Susan. "Sleep well Jimmy. Dream of me."

That settled it. Clearly I was losing it. Susan never called me Jimmy, always James. Something wasn't right. In fact, nothing made any sense tonight. It was all moonlight and madness. I climbed out of the window, into the garden. I looked up at the stars. In spite of everything I'd seen, everything I'd done, I was still just a fucked-up teenage boy. All I'd ever really wanted was a peaceful life. Admittedly, a peaceful life and loads of money, but still. It looked like you couldn't have the money without a little drama.

I needed to clear my head. Almost automatically, I began the kata. I moved to my left, a low block, then strike, 90 degrees to my right. Block, strike, strike, move left. Left strike, forward, strike, front kick. High block, knee kick, side kick, chop. It cleared my mind. I felt like the power of the stars and the moon had entered my body. I was, for once, at peace with the world. I was Bruce Lee, the dragon, reincarnated with a business brain almost as powerful as my fists.

I'd rule the world one day.

I went through all my attack moves, over and over again. Lightning fists of fury, for speed. Straight punches, hooks and uppercuts. This was my life, my real life. Boxing and martial arts. I'd been working out for almost two hours when I heard a twig snap, and saw a shadow moving away from the tree. I was being watched. Probably one of my bodyguards or my shadow, Ling. At that moment, I didn't give a flying fuck. I climbed back into my room. I left the window open. Went and had a much-needed shower, wrapped a towel around my waist and opened a bottle of spring water. I walked back into my bedroom, drank half of the water, screwed the lid back on and said: "Enough of this cloak and dagger bullshit. What do you want?" Ling looked at me, smiled and said, "I think you know."

She stood up, took off her coat, then her dress, her knee-length black leather boots, and finally her panties and bra. She let her jet black hair down and stood before me naked. Wow. What a sight. Despite Janet's earlier visit, despite my almost two-hour workout, I knew exactly what I wanted. Time stood still. I stared at her beauty, turning over the options in my head.

One. Have sex with her. Two. Walk a 200-yard minefield, blindfolded. Three. Cut my rock hard dick off and give it to her dad. Either way, I was most certainly getting fucked.

I was 17 years old. I gave in to temptation.

Ling was incredible. In two lust-filled hours, she turned the boy into a man. Her hands, lips and tongue were as smooth and caressing as silk. She had amazing moves. She showed me how to please and satisfy her. She orgasmed over and over again. I'd never seen anything like it. She looked like she was in a frenzy, way, way out of control. Her eyes glazed, she writhed and bucked, clutching the sheets in her hands and arching her back like a gymnast. Afterwards, we lay still, glued together by lust. It felt natural, calm. Later, after showering and dressing, she said as she climbed out the window, "See you tomorrow, my love."

What the fuck had just happened? Was it a dream? No, the scratches on my back were real enough. I drifted off to sleep, a smile on my face. My arrangement with Janet was over. She was no longer needed.

When I got up the next morning, I saw blood on the bedsheet. What the hell? Ling couldn't have been a virgin, she was just too good. Yes, it had been a tight fit, taking her that first time. But no, no way. Not with those moves. I guess we just fucked too hard. Fuck it, I'd buy a new sheet later. Right now, I was still in my happy bubble. Hi-ho, hi-ho, it's off to Ling I go... I showered and shaved in double quick time. Had to look my best. The latest shop was opening this day, right in the heart of Italian Mafia territory. Happily oblivious to this fact, and to the product we were actually selling, a dimwit local councillor cut the ribbon and unveiled the new sign above our shop. The Candy Man.

We'd spent a large chunk of money advertising. A flock of people entered the building. The tills rang loud all day, music to my ears. The fudge was rocketing out the door, along with our other products. My plan looked achievable — a shop in every town in the UK. London first, then outwards. I was already making four to five grand a week, cash. People will tell you crime doesn't pay. Trust me, it fucking does. I was living proof.

Chapter 12

Life could have been different if I'd listened to good advice. I could have built a career as a boxer, gone to the Olympics, gained fortune and fame in the noble art of fisticuffs. Who listens to good advice at 15 years old? I thought I was invincible. I was unbeaten in the ring. I'd knocked out every opponent, barely taken a slap myself. I put on a good performance, every time. I didn't beat my opponents. I broke them, destroyed them. So what if some old, past it, has-beens or never-weres thought I went in too hard? So what if they said I was savage? What did they know? I owned the ring. It was my stage, my show, my theatre.

My 6th amateur boxing match. Lots of influential people watching. Good performance a must. Three rounds. Ding ding. Round one.

My opponent danced across the ring, full of confidence. Started throwing punches at my head. No subtlety there, he was just trying to knock my block off. Noble art? Yeah, right. This was war. I dodged and ducked, avoiding his haymakers easily. A swift 1-2-3 to his unguarded ribcage, then a hard left hook to his liver and he buckled, presenting his chin as a perfect target. A short uppercut, right on the button, and a big right hook to his temple. He went down.

I watched and waited from a neutral corner. This kid was no match for me, but give him his due, he got up. He should have stayed down. The ref, dumb fuck, gave him a standing eight-count. Should have stopped the fight right there. The guy was clearly outclassed. He was going to get hurt. In the ref's shoes, I'd have given him a chance to bow out with dignity. What was this clown thinking? No time to wonder. The ref brushed the poor fucker's gloves off and in he came again.

Not good. I was angry. I could hear that violent little voice urging me on. This poor kid, just trying to do the same thing as me, was about to feel the full force of all that aggression, all that rage. I smashed punch after punch into his face, now completely covered in blood. Only the ropes were holding him up. The fucking sawdust-for-brains ref should have stepped in. His corner should have thrown in the towel. This wasn't boxing, it was slaughter.

He tried to cover up, I kept hitting. His arms dropped, I kept hitting. I only stopped when I heard the bell, more an automatic reaction than a desire to follow the rules. I walked back to my corner and sat on the wooden stool. My trainer was yelling. "Just finish the fucking fight, James! Stop fucking about, you hear me?"

See, right there. Right there is where I should have listened. I never listened to anyone. I had other ideas. I just shrugged, sipped some water and said, "He's one tough cookie." Gum shield back in. Round two. He was back on the canvas in less than a minute. Weak. Both eyes swollen up. Blood coming from his nose. He was fucked. The crowd wanted a battle, so I gave them one. Stepped back, let him get up, even swing a couple of punches before knocking him down again. He was saved, once more, by the bell.

My trainer didn't say a word this time. No point. Just waited in silence for the inevitable end. Knock out. Ding, ding...

I went in for the kill, unleashing an avalanche of blows that forced him against the ropes almost immediately. Full power shot to the head. Left hook, right hook, left again. A hard uppercut to his chin and two straight punches to the nose. From the corner of my eye, a flash of white. His trainer had finally thrown in the towel. I couldn't stop myself. I hit him one last time before the ref could reach me, putting all the fury I'd ever felt into the blow. He was out before he hit the canvas.

A human can only take so much punishment. The boy never regained consciousness. Spent two weeks in a coma on a life support machine before giving up completely. It was all over the news, the papers. My hopes of making the Olympic team were over, no way the committee would select me now. I was never even allowed to box for my club again, although they let me keep training. My dream of getting to the top needed a new direction.

Chapter 13

Time goes so fast. Somewhere in between constant working, training and sex with Ling, I reached my 18th birthday.

I got up extra early and went for a five-mile run. I got back, showered, shaved, had my final home cooked breakfast. Maybe this year would actually be a happy birthday. It's for sure it couldn't be worse than the other 17. I spoke to the kind couple who ran the youth home, thanked them both for looking after me. They'd actually got me a card and a gift — a book about boxing legends. I was genuinely touched. I'd got them presents too. A £100 department store gift card for her, a bottle of finest malt for him. I actually felt almost sad, leaving them. They were good people. I was officially an adult. It was time to get a great big fuck-off key for my own personal door.

My bags, such as they were, were packed, my driver and bodyguards were waiting. We loaded the car, went to a hotel. I checked in. A temporary measure until I'd found my perfect home.

Then we drove to the shop. The best present I could wish for was a peaceful, drama-free day. And it was. But fuck, I was so bored. We packed the online orders. Pottered about with the window display. Stocked the shelves. Eventually, Ling popped out to run some kind of errand. Idly, I flicked through the emails on my phone. One was from the adoption people. My sister lived in London and was very interested in meeting me. Brilliant. My brother, on the other hand, had moved to the US and wasn't. Less brilliant.

Fuck him, I thought, reading the email again. Cold rage flooded through me. We were brothers, for fuck's sake. Why was he rejecting me? He'd made the wrong decision. I made a promise. "We'll meet one day, big brother. We really will."

Taking a deep breath, I went back to the shop. Minutes later, Ling bounced back in. She took me to the storeroom, away from prying eyes, smiled and kissed me. "You'll get your real present later, I have a surprise for you now," she said. "Happy birthday, my love."

She handed me a gift-wrapped box. It felt heavy. Certainly wasn't socks. The wrapping fell away to show a smooth wooden box. Inside, two steel handguns, a box of bullets and a twin shoulder holster. What a woman. She showed me how to load and hold the guns, how to release the concealed safety catch. "These will keep you safe," she said. She didn't say from who. I thanked her. I smiled. Best present ever.

"We're meeting my father at eight tonight," she went on. Okay, that's pretty much a command. No training for me tonight, no chance to start looking for a home. But hey, I could still have ten minutes of me time on my 18th birthday. I went out to the back yard behind the shop. The sun was shining, warm on my face. I closed my eyes, tipped my head back. Slipped into the now-familiar daydream. Over the last few weeks, Ling had got into the dream. My wife, in my beautiful home. I should marry her, that much seemed clear. And that didn't trouble me. With Ling, things were straightforward, no drama. In my mind, I was ready to tell her Dad we were a couple. He would either like the news, or he could go fuck himself. I wasn't scared of him. Of anyone.

Ling's footsteps followed me into the yard. She leaned over and kissed me. I decided it was time to do something different today. Something just for us. "Let's go out to lunch," I said. She looked surprised, but didn't stop me as I took her hand and walked through the shop to my Merc. "Find us a nice quiet pub with decent food, please," I said. I wanted to be normal for a couple of hours. To be like any other 18-year-old, showing off my girlfriend to the world.

We stopped outside a real old pub, oozing Victorian charm. We went in, got drinks, ordered food, sat in the beer garden. Chatted, like a normal couple. Enjoyed a peaceful lunch. I felt fantastic. The real world, the one where the Mafia knew we were drug dealing on their turf and we were about to launch two new shops in Russian and Albanian territory, could wait.

After a couple of stolen hours in the sunshine, Ling and I made our way back to close up. As always, the day's takings went into two piles, one for Ling and one for me. We moved on to the second shop. As we turned into the road, Ling ordered: "Stop the car."

There was a black BMW parked outside our shop, back door open. We watched three men exit the shop, get in and drive away. They'd left the shop door ajar. "Okay," said Ling. "Drive on."

We parked and went inside. The manager and two saleswomen were definitely dead. Bullets to the brain normally work. The shop had been smashed up. We went out the back. The two women who made the fudge were also dead, also shot through the head. I checked the tills and safe. The money was still there. I put it in my bag and we went back to the car.

"Why'd you let them get away?" I asked. "We have to be careful, James," she said. "The police aren't fools. They're just waiting for us to make a mistake."

"A mistake?" I snarled. "There are five dead bodies in there, for fuck's sake!"

"Yes," she answered. "Why add three more to deal with?"

Ling made a call to her dad. A clean-up operation was needed, fast. The Triads had a deal with the local crematorium. Our dead people would be quietly cremated, their ashes sent back to China. All neat and tidy. All worked out.

It had to have been the Italians. A message. We waited by the shop until Ling's brother, Zen, rolled up, his men with him. He barked orders. The men fanned out, their grim mission already under way. Then our convoy of cars went back to Chinatown, back to our first shop. Ling, Zen and I went inside, the two of them arguing. I left them to it, went and got my guns. Took my jacket off, put on the shoulder holster. Double-checked both guns were loaded, safety catches on. Put them in the holsters. I was ready. I'd hunt them down and kill them all. Smash up my shop? Bastards.

Ling and Zen had stopped their heated discussion, were watching me. He finally turned on his heel, fucked off. Peace at last. Ling spoke quietly, telling me her dad's instructions. We went to the hotel, got my bags, checked out. "What's in the hold alls?" asked Ling.

"Cash," I replied, as the guys loaded them into the car.

 "How much?"

"No fucking clue."

<hr>

Chapter 14

We drove back to Chinatown, stopping by a narrow alleyway. I followed Ling along it, to a reinforced steel security door. It was the crappy flat above the shop, we'd checked out before, to see if we could use it for storage. My mouth dropped open as we went through the door. It wasn't crappy any more. It had been done up, high-spec, all mod cons. It must have cost a mint. Ling put the key into my hand. "You stay here now," she said. "It's safe. Your new home. A gift from my father. Happy birthday, James." She kissed me, and added, "I'll be back later."

This was amazing. My own pad, at long last. I let the hired help carry my bags up the stairs. Went into the bedroom, lay on my new, king-size bed, closed my tired eyes. I guess I drifted off, because the next thing I knew, the steel door was creaking open.

"It's only me!" Ling's voice. Fuck, she had a key. Why? I was starting to ask questions, to wonder if my life was being planned out by Ling, her dad and the Triad gang. Was I trapped? Did I care? Fuck it. I jumped in the shower, dressed in the clothes Ling had laid out for me. We went down to the Merc, drove the 300 yards to her dad's restaurant. Another little question — why didn't we walk?

We entered the eatery, minders close behind. Her Dad greeted me. A banner was taped up on the wall behind him: 'Happy 18th Birthday!' There were loads of people, a proper party, in fact. They'd gone to a lot of trouble. Why?

The Triad boss gave me a large envelope, clapping me on the shoulder, wishing me a happy birthday. I opened it. There was a large wad of cash inside. Then food was served, followed by a gigantic cake, complete with 18 candles. I was overwhelmed. I couldn't remember any birthday with a cake, not to mention a shower of gifts from people I hardly knew. Even Ling's brother had given me a cash-stuffed envelope. I smiled and smiled, thanked everyone enthusiastically. By the time the party was over, my face ached.

Sitting quietly in the now almost empty restaurant, Ling's Dad explained gang culture to me. If we chose to do nothing after the attack on our shop, that was a sign of weakness. So Zen had planned a raid. A show of strength and power. The Triads would strike back. And I was in it up to my neck. Fine by me. Payback was well deserved. Ling, Zen, me, a driver and eight gang members set off. No car this time. We sat on the floor in the back of a Transit van. Three Mercs would follow at a safe distance, as back-up.

The sub-machine gun felt reassuring. Our targets were the Italian storage facility and their main offices, down by the docks. We were tooled up and ready. So Zen said.

Silver sparkles from the clear bright moon cascaded across the Thames as we drove to the docks. It was 11.30pm. Quiet. Not for long. Ling, Zen and I jumped out of the van and ran to the warehouse. The others went towards a different building. This was shaping up to be another memorable birthday. I flicked my safety catch off and kicked the warehouse door open. Three startled security guards looked like rabbits in the headlights of a lorry. I opened fire, nearly cut them in half. Ling and Zen took care of three others who'd been playing cards at the back of the warehouse. Zen set up the finishing blow — literally. Explosives, set to go off in five minutes. Just enough time for us to get away.

On the other attack front, a fierce gun battle was in full flow. We circled around, caught our enemies off guard. Killed them all. I felt nothing. No remorse, no guilt. Just the mighty rush of adrenalin and the thought that it was all so easy. More explosives were set. We ran back to the van, got in just as the first building blew. The force of the blast flipped us onto our side. Fuck, not the plan. Way too many explosives had been used. We scrambled out, then the second building went up. Massive explosion. Down we all went again, glass and debris, bricks and dust flying past. Two of our men took hits. They stayed down, both with bad head wounds, bleeding heavily.

Ling's brother was also hit, not moving. What a fucking mess. Thank fuck the Merc driver saw the van go over and came screaming to the rescue. I picked up Ling and carried her to the car, screaming at the driver to get her in. Ran back and got Zen, although I'm not sure why I bothered. Fucking prick. I saw lights from vehicles. Heard shots. The Italian cavalry had arrived way earlier than we thought. Some of our guys were returning fire. I stumbled back to the Merc, threw Zen in, fell into the passenger seat. Yelled at the driver to move.

As he took off, I hit the horn and shouted to the others, sounding the retreat. We were outnumbered. Time to get out. Bullets still rained down like massive, deadly hailstones. Ling and Zen were both shot up. I picked up my sub-machine gun, leaned out of the window and let rip towards my targets. Only two of our men had survived, came careering towards the car. The rest lay dead. This was a fucking nightmare. Nice planning, Zen.

I felt a punch to my arm, knocking me backward into the car. A sting across my forehead. I'd been hit, once in the arm, once just glancing past my head, now that was a close shave. The car screeched to a shaky halt. I looked at the driver. No close shave for him. Dead. I got out, felt OK. Too bloody angry not to be. "Come on, you fuckers!" I screamed, as much to our retreating men as our enemies, firing the gun as I ran round the car. Dragged the dead driver out and jumped in his wet, bloody seat. Our survivors made it too, one scrambling into the back, one into the still-open passenger door.

I drove off, tires screeching on the tarmac. The Italians were in hot pursuit. We were in deep trouble. Time for action. I got up to 60mph, then braked hard. Two seconds later, the first chaser hit us. Caught a quick glimpse of two bloodied foreheads as I skidded into a doughnut and shot back towards the fire-engulfed buildings and the second chasing car. Hit it head on. Big crash. I was ready, braced. They were not. Two down. I pulled out one of my guns and shot the airbag, clearing my line of vision. Backed up, then drove off around the wreck. Idiots should have known Fiats weren't going to work in a car chase.

More shots coming at us. I took another hit. Fuck. No option. I drove into the burning warehouse, put my foot down hard, pedal to the metal and hoping for the best. I didn't know what else to do.

They had an army. Total madness for us to attack with so few men, without a backup plan. I drove through the flame-ravaged building and out into the darkness.

We shot across a ramp, just missed the huge dock crane. Then the car was flying. A moment of silence that seemed to last hours. Then the river. Huge impact. Water flooding in. I reached back — Ling was already moving, already squeezing through the shot-out rear screen. She could move enough to tread water. The two Triads were out and making their way to support her. I focused on Zen, diving under to drag him from the rapidly-sinking car. It took forever to drag his limp body to the surface. Breaking the water, I heard sirens. No matter, they'd focus on the bloodbath at the warehouse for a while.

Together, me supporting Ling and our men dragging her brother, we started swimming. It was a long way. When you're in trouble, you dig deep. Survival instinct kicks in, gives you the strength to do what you have to do, to stay alive. This, now, was the deepest I'd ever dug. It took everything I had, and a bit more. How we got across, I don't actually know. I was exhausted and so, so cold. Eventually, we made it to a moored boat. I didn't have the strength to haul myself up. I was holding on for dear life, holding onto Ling. The other two had some strength left. They clambered aboard, then dragged us after, Ling first, then Zen, then me. We staggered off the boat, up the stone steps to the dock. Dry land never felt so good.

One of the men went to find a pay phone and call for help. Five minutes later, our two backup Mercs roared up. Back to Chinatown, back to safety. I looked at the blood streaming from my arm, Ling's too. And her leg. Her prick of a brother had been hit in his stomach, too. He was already unconscious. We tried the best we could to stop the bleeding. But we'd lost too much blood ourselves. One by one, we passed out.

I came round to the smiling face of a Chinese surgeon. He was holding a stainless steel bowl with six bullets in it. He told me I was a lucky young man, and gave me the bullets. Oh yeah. Happy Birthday to me. We'd all made it through, even Zen, the mastermind behind the whole fucking mess. Ling's dad paid me a visit, grateful once again that I'd saved his loved ones. He had another plan. Jesus. He was running my life for me. But right then, right at that point, I was past caring. I'd go along with his plan.

Chapter 15

Five days later, Ling and I stepped off the family's private jet onto the tarmac in Hami Airport, Xinjiang. First time I'd ever been abroad. We were fast-tracked through customs, forged passports stamped, forged visas approved for an unlimited stay. Money talks, for sure, and here it had been shouting. It dawned on me, really dawned on me, how much power and influence Ling's father actually had. A convoy of five cars took us to our new home on the outskirts of the city.

My jaw dropped as we drove up. It was a palace. A fucking palace. And we were greeted like royalty, right enough. Ling's mum opened her arms to me, gave me a huge hug, then ordered some servants — servants! — to show me to my room. I'd never seen anything like it. Simply designed but so elegant. No flash here. You don't need it when you've got massive windows revealing incredible countryside and mountains that look like you could reach out and touch them. Perfect in every way.

I was tired from the long flight. Knowing Ling was as safe as houses here, I decided to chill out in style. After a quick shower I lay on the bed, shut my eyes. I caught the scent of Ling's perfume as she entered the room, walking as softly as a cat. She sat on the bed. I stayed still, breathing slow. Too tired to react, even to her. I felt her fingers brush my face, her lips touch my forehead, lightly, where there was still a brown scar from the bullet that had barely missed me. I heard her whisper, "I love you, James.

"I'll make you happy," she went on. "I'm yours, body and soul. My heart beats only for you. Only for you, until my last breath." She paused. I felt a warm, wet drop on my cheek. After a moment she added one more line, "You're the bravest man I've ever met."

Then she got up. I heard the door latch click. Her words echoed and floated around the room. My bamboozled brain didn't know what to think. I liked Ling. Liked her a lot. Beautiful, smart, brave, fierce, sexy as hell. All pros. Ruthless. Reckless. Crazy. Borderline homicidal, at times. Not to mention daughter of, it was becoming clearer all the time, one of the most powerful gang bosses in the world. Cons? Jury's still out.

Each day in this almost magical place, protected by mountains, surrounded by silence, I felt better. My wounds were healing. Ling was mending too. We spent most of our time together, just the two of us. We walked, hand in hand, around the gardens and, gradually, through the countryside, even up into the foothills of those mountains. Just like a normal couple. I was amazed when Ling suggested we start training again. We?

Turned out she'd been trained, from an early age, in a unique system of martial arts, not one that was — or could ever be — taught in the western world. It incorporated an extremely secret and lethal method, Dim Mak, as well as the ancient Shaolin Kung Fu. Dim Mak, the 'death touch', was fascinating. It focused on vital points on an enemy's body. Hit those points hard enough, and the heart would stop instantly. The more Ling taught me, the more I wanted to learn. We trained together most days.

As the days flew by, I learned new skills. How to handle various armaments: handguns, rifles, machine guns, swords, daggers. How to shoot straight over long distances. How to disassemble, clean and reassemble various weapons of death. I practiced everything, every day, sometimes with modern weapons, sometimes on ancient arts.

Ling introduced me to her original instructor, an old monk in the Shaolin temple, high up on the mountain. He taught me moves I'd never seen before. I absorbed it all, like a sponge in water. After a few weeks, Ling and I agreed to live there for a few months, becoming part of the community, training like never before. This old monk was a Grand Master. He'd dedicated his whole life to the martial arts. He gave me a sword and showed me how to use it. A katana, a true, handcrafted, Japanese Samurai sword. How it came to be in the temple, I never asked. Most likely some unfortunate Japanese invader had it with him when he chose to attack the wrong group of monks.

Six months later, we'd completed our Dim Mak and Kung Fu training. That evening we went home. We showered together, had hard, fast, fantastic sex. Training requires celibacy. We made up for lost time in a big hurry.

We'd made a decision at the temple. We stopped trying to hide our relationship. We were out in the open, no sneaking around. We shared a room. I was, for the first time in my life, at peace. Given the choice, I'd have stayed in China. Forever.

One morning, bright and early, Ling zoomed onto our bed, her phone in her outstretched hand. She handed it to me. We'd spoken about this very important call the night before. It was her Dad. News had filtered back to the UK about us. Speaking without emotion, he said, "I think, young man, you have something to ask me?" I looked at Ling. We needed his blessing or it was a no go. Smiling, I asked:,"May I marry your daughter, sir?"

Chapter 16

The following day, a tattoo artist came to the fortress. He gave me one on my neck, one on my upper left arm. Dragons. I swore the oath of allegiance, and became an official member of the Dragon Triads. The wedding date was set. Ling's dad would be flying over, her brother too. His reaction was going to be interesting.

The day of our engagement party, the Grand Master came down from the temple. After watching us go through a 30-minute form, done in perfect synchrony, he handed both of us a gold sash embroidered with a dragon. As I received his gift, I realised something. It was my 19th birthday. And I hadn't killed anyone in a whole year.

Later, at our engagement party, more gifts. It's a crazy world. We were sitting in the lap of luxury, both of us rich beyond counting, and people were handing us envelopes filled with cash. Funny how that works. When I had nothing, no-one wanted to know. Now I was rolling in money, and everyone wanted to give me more. Still. The food was delicious, and I spent the evening with Grand Master while a small orchestra played traditional Chinese music. I was content. No violence, no voices in my head. No drama. Life was pretty amazing.

Another year flew by. I'd never known it was possible to be this content. Together, Ling and I explored Hami, an incredible city, a blend of the historical and modern, of Chinese and Uyghur cultures and more. We tasted the sweet melons in the marketplaces. Admired the beauty of the city's architecture. Occasionally we went out into the countryside, among endless fields rippling in the breeze, or into the desert to visit the weird rock formations known as 'Demon City'.

My 20th birthday was our wedding day. It was a grand affair, a massive parade of wealth. Not my choice, but I went along with it to please Ling and her mother. Huge guest list. Massive marquee on the lawns. Army of catering and serving staff. An orchestra for the ceremony, a live band for the reception. Peacocks, actual peacocks, strutting about the grounds, making that godawful noise they make. Money no object. All wasted on me. Because all I could see was Ling, her white designer dress showing off her beautiful body and glorious jet-black hair, coming towards me on her father's arm.

I had a brief moment of terrifying clarity as our marriage was pronounced. My wife was a Triad gang leader's daughter. And a pretty lethal gang member herself. Was I nuts? Too late now. Because if I ever tried to leave her, she'd fucking kill me.

Ceremony over, Ling's dad and I stepped into his study while the guests shuffled into the marquee for the outrageously large meal. He turned to me and said, as expected, "Look after my daughter. Treat her well, and all will be good between us." He didn't need to spell out what would happen if I didn't. He handed me an envelope. "My gift to the happy couple," he said. A cheque. A cheque for two million US dollars. I looked at him. He nodded, and smiled. "No need to thank," he said. "You are family now."

We spent our honeymoon in a log cabin on the side of the mountain. I smiled when I saw it, remembering an six-year-old self sharing a dream with an old man. "I'm going to rescue a princess, Grandpa. Rescue her and marry her and live in a big house on a mountain." And him telling me to go live that dream. Well, after two hedonistic weeks in that cabin, fucking and sucking and grabbing and groping in every way imaginable, it looked like I was taking his advice. This sure as hell seemed like a dream to me. Ling was gentle, kind and loving when it was just us two. She was quiet, at peace. So was I. Our whole focus was on making each other happy. And, in the back of my mind, her father's words constantly repeating, "You are family now."

Family.

That's what brought us back, in the end. I'd been in touch with a private investigator before I left. His mission was to find my long lost dad. If he was still alive, he'd be found. I wanted to look him in the eye and ask why he'd run away from his wife, his three kids. It tore me up every time I thought about it. Fucking coward.

Plus, I was desperate to meet my sister, Lisa. After the battle at the docks, it had all been put on hold. Now I had started my own family, it was time to make the connections with those I'd lost long ago. Despite that desire, though, I sighed as our jet touched down at Heathrow. I hadn't missed this life. I'd made the choice to come back. Stronger, fitter, smarter. And with a beautiful wife by my side. So there was nothing for it but to get on with business.

A driver and bodyguards met us at the airport with a new, top-of-the-range Merc, jet black. Suited my mood. We breezed through customs and back to Chinatown. So much had changed. Eight Candy Man shops now, all doing well. The accountant who'd taken charge while we were away briefed us on our drive from the airport. Turned out he was Ling's uncle. I guess I shouldn't have been surprised. He brought us up to speed. We were making a fortune on the fudge, outselling all the other leading brands. And that was the stuff without the drugs. Amazing. Who knew?

At a late supper with Ling's dad, the three of us talked into the night. Ling and I had new roles to play. We would continue to run the Chinatown shop, and collect the cash from the rest. We'd also lead the gang war.

The other gangs were trying to protect their own businesses, heavily dependent on drug money. Russians, Italians, Jamaicans, Albanians, even other, smaller Chinese gangs. Ling and I went on a highly-organised killing spree. I dropped a bag of candy at each site, sending a message: cross us, you make the hit list. These were, as they say, interesting times. A lot of them died. A lot of ours died, too. But for me, it was just going through the motions. I was already stinking rich, so what was it all for? All I really wanted was to connect with my family — my whole family — and settle down into a peaceful life.

•

Chapter 17

Finally, on a beautiful late autumn afternoon, I met my sister. Lisa. 22 years old, just finished a law degree. So beautiful, just like the picture I carried in my head of my mum. Tall, athletic, long dark hair. My eyes. Not married, no kids. About to start work with a firm of solicitors and begin paying off the debts she'd built up over four years at uni. We sat over coffee, talked and talked. So many questions. So few answers.

I could tell her about the shops, not the real nature of the business. About my wife, not her connections. About me, but not the whole me. Not the dark me, the killer me, the one with the quietly violent voice in his head. She could tell me about her family, but not mine. The people who adopted her had given her a good life. She didn't remember our parents, or our brother – she'd only been two years old when we were separated.

Still, it was a great afternoon. I'd brought her a gift — a white gold friendship bracelet. She thanked me, gave me a massive hug — fuck, what an incredible moment. My sister, hugging me. It felt like something broken suddenly healed. We sat and chatted in the sunshine for two hours, before exchanging numbers and agreeing our next date to meet. I want back to the flat a very happy guy. I'd start a search in the new year, looking for a family home for Lisa, Ling and me.

On our next meet, I gave her an envelope of cash. She didn't want to take it, I insisted. I told her our real Mum would be proud of her, that I was too. That I was happy I could help out. It was only money, I said. I had plenty. And I wanted to share it with my sister. After lunch, I took Lisa back to the flat, showed her the shop, introduced her to Ling, and her dad. We ate at the restaurant, Ling's dad playing the perfect, twinkly, Old-Chinese-gentleman host. Later, back at the flat, the three of us talked late into the night. Lisa stayed in the guest room. Honestly, best day of my life.

We met up every week for the next few weeks. She told her adoptive parents about me, invited me to meet them. I paid off her debts. She fought me on that, but I won. I didn't care about the money. I cared about my sister. I wanted her to focus on her career, not her debts. Not when I could clear them without blinking. So she accepted, tearfully but with a big smile on her face all the same. "Hey," I said, "It's what mum would want. It's how it would have been if we'd never been separated. Don't even give it another thought."

Christmas was right around the corner. Lisa's parents had invited me for Christmas dinner, and I accepted. An actual, old-fashioned, family Christmas dinner. Wow. A first for me. Ling declined. She'd spend the day with her dad and brother while I got to know my new extended family.

Meantime, Lisa, Ling and me went shopping. Surprising how much fun it was, with the two of them by my side. On Christmas Eve, Ling and Lisa spent the day together while I worked flat out in the shop. After closing up and doing my rounds to collect and deliver the cash, I went back to the flat.

There was a huge tree in one corner, a pile of presents underneath. Tinsel all over the place, tacky as hell but so funny. Lights dancing and flickering around the tree, the windows, the fireplace, everywhere. And, standing in front of it all, grinning, my sister and my wife.

Ling had brought in food from the restaurant. We ate till we were bursting, then swapped gifts. A Rolex for Lisa from Ling and me. Diamond pendants on white gold chains from me to each of them. Amazing hand-made solid-gold cufflinks from Lisa to me. And, my personal favourite, a hideous pair of Christmas socks with a little button that played a horrible tinny version of 'Jingle Bells' while a red-nosed Rudolph grinned up from my toes.

Then we watched a movie, just like any other normal family spending a happy Christmas Eve together. It was fantastic. I was so happy. Lisa stayed the night.

Next day, Lisa and I went to her family's home in the chauffeur-driven Merc. I was a little nervous. Weird. The things I'd done without even thinking about it, and Christmas Day with my sister and her family made me nervous. The warm and sincere welcome from Lisa's mum and dad sorted it out almost immediately. I gave them both a small gift and a bottle of champagne. The day went well — a wonderful meal, good company, a happy family. It just didn't get any better.

Two days later, Ling and I stood outside an Italian restaurant. The place was packed. The Boss's birthday party. We'd watched the punters go in. Men, women, little kids. Unimportant details. Payback.

I screwed the silencer onto my gun, got out of the Merc and walked to the door, shooting the two minders on either side point blank. Ling handed me my submachine gun. I smiled as we went inside, opened fire. Blasted anything that moved — even the fish in the gaudy tank over the counter. I dropped two grenades as we walked into the kitchen, Ling still shooting. Then I dropped two bags of candy as we went out the back door. Revenge complete. It might have taken two years. The people who'd shot my staff and smashed up my shop had paid in blood.

Next day's news: 60 people dead, massacred by The Candy Man.

●

Chapter 18

The rest of the week went fast. New Year's Eve, Ling and I went to the restaurant for a quiet meal. No partying for us, a quiet night at home was all we needed. Halfway through watching some crappy movie or other, Ling's phone buzzed. She put the call on speaker. One of the Triad clubs had been hit. There was a Merc outside, ready to take us to the scene.

The place had been shut and cordoned off by the police. We couldn't get near. Then my phone lit up. It was Lisa's adoptive dad. He was at the hospital, asked me to get there ASAP. Ling saw my face. "What's up, James? James?" I told her. We drove to the hospital together, then I sent her home. I ran to A and E, half out of my mind. Lisa's folks were there, looking worried. Her dad told me what he knew. Fuck.

"She went to the club with her friends," he said. They'd been waiting outside for the doors to open, standing in the VIP queue. There was a drive-by, or something, we're not sure, they were all hit." He stopped, gulped back tears. "Her friends... they didn't make it," he managed to go on. "And Lisa... Lisa's in surgery. It doesn't... Well, it doesn't look good, James."

He couldn't go on. I couldn't answer. This was all my fault. I gave her VIP tickets. We all sat in the waiting room in silence. I prayed for the first time in my life. Prayed for Lisa to live. Prayed that somehow this wasn't my fault. Even managed to pray for her parents, somewhere in there. On the waiting room TV, the horror played out over and over again.

Six hours we sat there before a surgeon came to see us. As he spoke, I felt like I could breathe again. They'd managed to save my sister's life. She was stable and the surgeon was confident she'd make a full recovery. I phoned Ling, shared the good news. She was almost as relieved as I was.

Two hours later, by the side of Lisa's bed in a private room. I sat listening to the beep-beep-beep of the monitors. Lisa was alive. I held her hand. I had to keep her that way. I had to make plans. I went back to Chinatown and met Ling and her dad at the restaurant. I told him what I wanted to do, asked for his help. "No problem," he replied. Just like that. I hoped Lisa and her parents would understand. It was the best way, the only way to protect her.

Next day, showered and shaved, I went back to the hospital. Lisa's parents were there. She'd been awake, they told me, drunk some water. Now she was sleeping again. Quietly, I went into her room. She looked like an angel. I clenched my fists. I had to protect her. I'd give my life to do that. I told her parents about my plan. "Trust me," I said. "It'll help her. And it'll be safe. I'll make sure of it."

Two weeks later, Lisa had the all clear to travel. The jet was fuelled and ready. Lisa, Ling and me were on the way back to China. Lisa was physically doing really well. China and me, we'd sort out her mental health. I took her up the mountain, to the cabin where I'd spent my honeymoon with Ling. She loved it, like I knew she would. The quiet, the tranquillity, the safety of this magical place would help her to heal.

One warm day we sat outside, a picnic of delicate little treats all around us. We'd been talking for hours, absorbing the views. Just Lisa and me, Ling was at home with her mother. As the sun went down, we walked to the edge of the cliff face. I took her hand. "You're safe here, angel," I said. "No-one is ever going to hurt you again." I'd never felt so close, so connected to anyone.

Bright and early the next morning, over breakfast, I decided the time had come. Lisa deserved the truth. I started by showing her my martial arts book, the book that had belonged to our mother and that I still took with me everywhere. She was the only other person ever to see inside it. Ever, since my teacher, to see the drawing I'd stuck inside it all those years ago. She glanced up at me, touching the image of our father, surrounded by flames, a sword sticking through his chest.

"What happened, James?" she said. "Why did he run away?"

"Because he was a fucking coward," I spat. "And a fucking thief. He stole from us. All those years we could have been together. If he's still alive, I'm going to track him down. I'm going to make him pay."

She was looking at me with a mix of fear and wonder. This was it. Now or never. I told her everything. The shops. The drugs. The threat of other gangs. Why she had to trust me now. Why only I could really keep her safe. She was silent for a long, long time. For a moment I thought it was over, I'd lost her. Then she stood up, came round the table and hugged me. Just hugged me. We stayed that way for ages. Eventually, I gently pushed her away. "It's time," I said. "Let's crack on."

We went back to the grand family home. An hour afterwards, clean and refreshed, we went into town, where I bought her everything she was going to need for the next six months. Back at the house, we packed a rucksack each. Then we started a long, uphill trek. Her injuries were so well healed, we made it in just under three hours. I banged on the huge oak gate. It swung open. "Welcome," said Grand Master, bowing in greeting. "I've been expecting you."

Lisa was going to remain at the temple, learning how to defend herself. She'd be safe, there were over fifty monks, all skilled in deadly martial arts, there to protect her. Along with six full-time bodyguards. I wasn't taking any chances. When she'd completed her training, she'd begin a career with the family law firm here in China. We'd fly her parents out to visit whenever they wanted. It was a fresh start. A new life. Safe.

Chapter 19

Back to London, and personal business to take care of. We knew the Russians were behind the attack on the club. Ling's dad and brother listened as I told them what the shooters had in store. They didn't give a fuck about my sister, so I left her out of it. Focused on the money and power, the expansion prospects if the plan worked. I'd chosen our targets, laid everything out clearly. The Candy Man was going to strike hard.

With 30 heavily-armed gang members, we took them by surprise in a long night of slaughter. First, their warehouse at the docks. 20 dead. Eyes out, ears off, throats slit. Shoot my sister, you fucking die. On to their minicab office. I stood outside, sub-machine gun ready, shouted "Fire!" The bullets ripped. I stepped into hell, fired at close range to finish the job. Another 15 dead.

My men went to clear the rest of the building. One passed me a hammer. I pulverized three dead guys' heads, flattened like pancakes. I was in a frenzy. Total madness. Total revenge.

As I dropped the bags of candy, we heard the sirens. Time to move on.

We stopped 200 yards from the home of the Russian gang boss. I deployed half my men to attack from the back. I spotted two guards at the steel gates as our van rammed through. We followed, not sure how many others were at the house. The battle was short and sweet as hell. My guys did their jobs well. When I walked into the house the boss, the top Russian guy in the UK was tied up, on his knees, wife and two kids tied, by his side. All was good.

I shot the kids first. One bullet to each of their heads. I tore his wife's nightie off, put the gun to her lips and said "Open wide." I forced the gun in her mouth, looked at her husband. "You fucked with The Candy Man," I said, as I squeezed the trigger. Then I pushed the Russian over, pointed my gun at his head and fired. He wasn't going to tell anyone anything. Dead men can't talk.

The guys poured petrol, I lit the fire. Back to the vans, reloading as we travelled to their brothel, the place most of them hung out. Fuck it, if you're going through hell, keep going. We stormed the building. Five minutes of terror later, dead bodies lay all around. Men and women both, no-one lived to tell the tale. One Russian guy lay wounded, caught with his trousers down, fucking a whore. I opened my flick knife, screaming: "I'm the Candy Man, don't fuck with me!"

It took five guys to pull me off him. Life in the fast lane.

I stared at Ling's brother, then calm again in an instant. "Let's go get something to eat," I said. "I'm famished."

Only four of our gang didn't make it. We'd wiped out, in one crazy night, the largest Russian gang in London. A good night's work. I did it for my sister, for revenge. They did it for the Russian's turf. We all knew the Russians would eventually regroup and come back at us. For now, back at the restaurant, Ling's dad was a happy man.

I ate, drank coffee, went back to my flat with my wife. I stared in disbelief at my reflection in the window. I looked like a vampire, bloody from head to toe. I took off my soaked shirt and trousers. Washed the blood from my hands, face, and body, in the shower. Cleansed, baptized of all my sins.

The months rolled on. I kept my head down until my 21st birthday came around. Another day nearly over. At 6 pm, we locked the shop and I went for a run. Three miles in, I stopped and checked my watch. Time for more personal revenge. I saw the woman walking towards me. Put my hood up, pulled my gun out and shot her three times. The bitch from the adoption agency wouldn't be breaking up any more families. I walked away, then turned a corner and jogged home.

Back at the flat, I showered and tried to shave. I stared in the bathroom mirror. A stranger stared back, hollow-eyed, blank-faced. I raised my fist and smashed the glass. I fucking hated that guy. He'd ruined my dream, my chance for a normal life. I was so angry. Ling heard the noise and came in. She looked at my hand, quietly fetched a bandage and dressed the wounds. Kissed me softly on the side of my jaw, then led me to the bedroom, where my clothes were laid out, ready for dinner with her family. Red tie, black suit, white shirt, black brogues, highly polished.

We went to the restaurant. Just the four of us. Ling, me, her dad and Zen. A last supper. I wasn't feeling good about it. Her dad was retiring. Going back to China. Which made Zen the new boss.

He wanted Ling to travel back to China with her dad. "If Ling's going, I'm going too," I said. "I'm her husband." His quick temper flared. No self-control. "She goes, you stay!" he yelled, running a finger across his throat. I looked at Ling's dad. He kept silent. So would I. Zen stared, hatred blazing. He hated me because I wasn't scared of him. Wasn't one of them, wasn't Chinese. Was married to his sister. He could go and fuck himself. Ling spoke. "I will obey your wishes, my brother."

Zen turned sharply and went on his way. Didn't even wish me a happy birthday. Why did Ling love this guy? He was a fucking prick. I sighed, "It'll all work out for the best, I guess." As I kissed her, my anger subsided. I wanted to go with her. I wanted to see my sister. I missed her like crazy. I'd bide my time.

We sat for the rest of the evening, talking with her old dad. He spoke quietly about the family business interests in China. It blew my mind. This was different league. He'd built an entire empire all by himself. Brick by brick. Fucking hell. "You have all that," I said. "Why did you want the shops, too?"

"I didn't want them, you did." he replied. He had a valid point. He'd done it for me. Simple as that.

He was happy I'd be staying in the UK. To keep an eye on the family business, he said. He knew his son was a fool.

They were flying out the next morning. Ling and I spent the night glued together. Next day, I went with them to the airport. "Be strong," I said, holding my wife. "Stay safe. And give Lisa a hug from me." I turned to her dad and shook his hand. I could barely get out the words to thank him. "No need," he said, holding my hand in both of his. "You're the son I wanted."

I never spoke to him again. Two things you are sure of in life, death and taxes. It's what you do right now that counts.

I missed Ling. Every night in an empty flat. I trained hard out in the yard behind the shop. I went to one of the triad-owned brothels twice a week. I needed sex. Perks of the job.

Chapter 20

Six months later, we got the phone call. Ling's dad had passed away peacefully, at home, where he'd chosen to be. I went to the funeral. Wanted to pay my respects. I flew commercial, wasn't sharing that flight with Zen, even for the luxuries of a private jet.

It was like a state funeral, streets lined with people paying their respects. Must have been the whole population of the town. Even the Grand Master and the monks from the temple were there. In fact, some of the monks carried the coffin. We stopped at a small temple in the town. A short service, then on to the cemetery. I stood next to my wife, held her hand tight. Lisa stood the other side, holding my other hand. The coffin was lowered, the neatly dug grave filled in.

Back at the mansion, I sat in a corner of the room with Lisa. She'd finished her training, fallen in love with her new home. Ling's dad, as he'd promised, had given her a job. And a tattoo. A dragon on her neck. My amazing sister.

That evening, we sat around the large dining room table, eating in silence. After we finished, I went quietly up to my old room. I lay on the bed, flicking through my book, thinking how different life could have been. When Ling came up, an hour later, she was crying, so sad. I put my book down, wrapped my arms around her. Nothing else I could do. We lay on the bed, silent. I listened to her breathing, felt her heartbeat. I thought about her father. What could I say? He was probably burning in hell. Ruthless, evil. He lived his life murdering those who stood in his way. He was all about money and power. Hard to see where the love was. Ling loved her dad. I hated mine.

Maybe he'd taken me under his wing because he saw the same things in me. That was a scary thought.

I stayed with Ling for a week. She'd travel back in a couple of months. She needed time to grieve with her mother. I'd wait. Meanwhile, I kept busy in the shop and trained hard. Jogged each day, going through my moves in the shop's back yard. I beat the crap out of my punch bag. By the time Ling returned, I was in the shape of my life.

Zen quickly tried to put a wedge between us. He put Ling in charge of the casino, the two clubs and the five brothels. It kept her very busy. I was on my own most nights. I stopped going to the restaurant. She'd come back to the flat at two or three in the morning, tired and sad. She was on autopilot. A brave face during the day. Crying herself to sleep at night. Her heart was broken. I still had hope. Ling would come back. She was strong. In the meantime, business came first. Time rolled on.

23rd birthday. Ling and I stood in an amazing penthouse apartment. There were two women cleaners laid to rest in the built-in wardrobes. A dead security guard neatly tucked behind his desk at reception. The smoking ruins of a couple of surveillance cameras scattered across the hallway. Ling and I opened our briefcases, and almost in unison, screwed our long-range rifles together. They'd been specially made in China, could be broken down in a heartbeat to fit in a briefcase. I smiled at my wife. She was ready.

Sliding one of the balcony doors open, I lay down, Ling next to me. I loaded my rifle, one bullet. Ling followed my lead. The sky clouded over, maybe a sign from above. A giant storm brewing. The wedding party came out of the church bang on time. We were 500 yards away, a perfect location. They gathered on the church steps for photos. I lined up my sights, slowed my breathing, tapped Ling's foot and quietly counted down. Five. Four. Three. Two. One. We fired at the same moment. The bride and groom folded up. We slid back into the penthouse, slowly closed the door, took our rifles apart and made for the lift. The Albanian gang boss and his new bride lay dead on the steps, surrounded by their screaming wedding guests. That's what happens when you firebomb a Candy Man shop.

Nothing personal, just business. At home, I took a shower. Dried off and joined Ling in our bed. We had fast, frantic sex, all the more intense these days because it happened less often. She fell asleep. Still restless, I had to clear my head. I slid out of the bed, into the living room. Moved into to my fighting stance, went through my moves, over and over again. When I was done, I took my sweaty clothes off, caught my reflection. One side of my body was covered in blood. I shook my head, blinked. Looked down. No blood. Great. Now I was losing my mind.

Ling went back to China a year later, at Zen's request, to care for her elderly mother. I took her to the airport. As instructed, that evening, I met Zen at the Chinese restaurant, sitting in his departed dad's chair, trying to wear his dad's shoes. He should have stuck with his own shoes, lost that terrible gold chain and medallion.

He spoke. "You'll go back to collecting the takings from the shops each day," he said. "You bring them here, to me, that's your job." He was making me an errand boy, a deliberate insult. I knew he was testing me, seeing how far he could push before I snapped. He had plenty of men to do this task. He could fuck off.

Before I could speak, one of his men placed some papers on the table. "Sign the papers," Zen said. "You not own half the shops any more. You get paid by me if you do your job." I looked at him for a minute. Smiled. I signed the papers willingly.

Fuck it. Fuck the shops and all the hassle. I had plenty of money, enough to last a lifetime. It was time for me to change my life. "Fine," I said. "I have other plans. I'm leaving. I leave a free man, not a dead man. Agreed?"

"Agreed," he said. He made a phone call, spoke in Chinese. I knew it didn't work that way. I knew far too much about the business, the drugs, the prostitution, the racketeering, the protection money, the people trafficking. The list was endless. Zen put down the phone, grinned at me. "Let's celebrate," he said. We sat around that table playing cards for two fucking wasted hours of my life. He drank too much, acting the fool, not the boss. One day, the walls were going to come in on him. As I got up to leave, he slapped me on the back and said, "You're a good man James! My brother! We are family!" Two-faced, lying bastard.

I walked out of the restaurant. The Merc, driver, and minders had disappeared in a puff of smoke. For the first time, I walked the 300 yards between the restaurant and the flat. My flat. My first real home. I had to leave it. Zen would never keep his word. He had no honour. He would undoubtedly try to kill me. You don't leave the Triads unless you're in a coffin.

A tramp was sleeping by the side of steel door, wrapped in the remains of a cardboard box for warmth. As I pushed the key in the lock, I felt the start of an electric tingle run up my spine. Survival instincts kicked in hard. I jumped back, leaving the key partly in the lock. Saw the thin wire across the door, both ends attached to sinister looking boxes. I stepped back, thinking fast. I kicked the tramp on his outstretched leg. He woke. He stank.

"Can you help me, please?" I said. "I can't get the door open. I'll give you fifty quid if you can." The tramp frowned, held his hand out. I gave him fifty quid, then dived for cover as he opened the door. I watched as the force of the explosion blew him across the alleyway. This was fast for Zen. I thought he'd wait at least a week or two.

I ran up the stairs through smoke and flames, grabbed the ever-ready holdall full of cash, along with my passport, and exited the burning building down the fire escape. Then I walked towards the restaurant. I pulled the collar of my coat up and sat down two doors away. The tramp's face had been blown up, his clothes and skin on fire. I hoped they'd think it was me. They must have heard the boom. I reached into my pockets, felt the reassuring cold steel of my guns. All loaded and ready for action. Another life changing moment. I felt calm, not angry.

20 minutes later, Zen came out with four bodyguards, all of them clearly a bit tipsy. Good for me. I jumped up and shot the bodyguards, stone dead in seconds. Then I shot Zen in the stomach, turned and shot the waiting driver in his head. Zen was on his knees, white shirt was soaked in blood. I knelt down beside him and said, "This could have been so different... brother." I saw the fear in his eyes before I hit him with another eight bullets to the head. I turned and walked into the night. Ling's uncle would be boss now. She was safe as houses, he loved her like a daughter. And she'd know it wasn't me who'd died. She knew I was immortal.

Chapter 21

On Monday morning, I strolled into a recruitment centre in Paris. I'd spent the weekend in a five-star hotel in the very pleasurable company of some five-star hookers. What the hell, I deserved a little R&R before beginning my new life. It was going to be a tough one. Not for the faint-hearted.

I'd bought a French phrase book, started reading on the Eurostar. I was going to have to learn the language. I was about to begin an entirely new chapter, one that, to be honest, even I hadn't seen coming. "This is what you really want?" said the man behind the desk. "It's what I really want," I replied. I smiled at the man. Game on.

I signed some forms, closed the deal. I was twenty-four years old, with no life plans in place. I needed somewhere to lie low, to bide my time. Somewhere I could assume a new identity, try a new kind of life, leave my past behind. So I joined the French Foreign Legion. Why? To see if I could. I knew they were an elite fighting unit. I knew the selection and basic training were among the toughest in the world. I knew it would make me or break me. I needed a challenge. And challenges don't get much bigger.

I thought life with the Shaolin monks might have given me some clue about military life. What a laugh. The first two weeks at the training centre in Aubagne, known for some reason as 'La Ferme' — the Farm — were flat out. Psychological and personality tests. A logic test. A medical examination, physical conditioning tests. All before selection was confirmed. I made it through, working hard, keeping my head down. Took — and obeyed — orders for the first time in my life. Excelled in unarmed combat and on the shooting range. Studied French, marched for hours, learned the legendary songs. All just a bit of fun. Something different. I learned a hell of a lot, about myself.

After six weeks of training, we did a 31-mile march, fully loaded with an 80-pound rucksack, over two days. That was tough. That almost broke the lot of us. It was nothing compared to the final test. 75 miles, full pack, over three days. The night before, one of my military brothers was sweating. "How the fuck are we going to do this?" he asked. "Just take the first step," I said. "Then keep going".

It was bad. Then it got worse. We went to the French Pyrenees for mountain conditioning. A week in the bitter cold, yomping through unforgiving terrain, nights when we thought we'd never be warm again. Finally, back to The Farm, where we'd be assigned to a regiment and operational duties. Of the 30 men who joined with me, only eight were left standing. There I was. I'd undertaken one of the world's toughest induction processes, and come through. I was officially a legionnaire. I felt a sense of pride, wearing the uniform.

My unit was sent to North Africa, peacekeeping troops under the umbrella of the United Nations. Me, keeping the peace. You have to laugh. Basically, we were cannon fodder. On patrol every day. Most days we engaged with the enemy — communist-backed 'freedom fighters'. Murdering terrorists, in my mind. There was one golden rule: don't fire at them until they fire at you. Crazy. How was I meant to do my job, to protect the innocent, if I couldn't just kill them all?

It came to a head when two of our men got themselves captured while they were out drinking. Local informers had told us who the kidnappers were and given us a location. You don't leave men behind in the Legion. There's people there from all over the world, different languages, different cultures. The one thing we all have in common? We're Legionnaires. That comes before anything else. Absolute loyalty, absolute commitment to your brothers in arms. Honneur et Fidélité. It was the only way.

Our mission was to get our men back. Our commanding officer, the adjudant-chef, who we simply called the AC — had briefed us. Minimum force. What a joke. We had a UN observer on board, so rules had to be seen to be obeyed. It was 11 pm, we were 500 yards away from our target. I surveyed the hideout through my rifle's telescopic sights. The UN observer was by my side. Protocol had to be followed, to the letter. We might as well give ourselves up. We'd seen so much bloodshed, so many deaths. It was a one-sided war, our hands were tied. Well, he could fuck off. I had a job to do. I was in charge of this raid, so I gave the orders. My men moved into position. At 23.30, we'd strike a blow for democracy. I told the UN official to keep his head down, then moved in for the kill. No prisoners tonight.

A knife in each hand, I silently took out the two guards, throats slit, down. I signalled the team into the compound. Shielded by darkness, we edged in. "Go, go, go," I whispered into the radio. Ten minutes later, the compound was secure. Five freedom fighters knelt on the ground, hands tied. Another twenty or so lay dead. Just numbers. The UN official was driving me mad, screaming about the Geneva convention. Fuck's sake. He gave me a headache.

We found our two fellow legionnaires in the basement. They were naked, hanging from a rafter by their feet. Their faces had been smashed up with hammers or rifle butts. They'd had their fingers hacked off, their bodies slashed like a patchwork quilt. Their severed dicks had been stuffed in their mouths. Three of the guys threw up. A gory sight.

I looked at the AC, then the UN observer. I held out my hands, like I was handcuffed. "Time to take the shackles off, for fuck's sake," I growled.

"Get them down from there," barked the AC. Behind him, the UN guy started bleating again. I saw the AC stiffen, then reach for an enemy handgun. He clicked back the safety catch. Then turned around and shot the fucker right through the skull. We dumped him in a body bag, a bit less respectfully than we handled our own dead. Then the prisoners were brought down.

We watched and waited. The AC picked up an old sword leaning against one of the blood-soaked walls. He pulled it out of its leather sheath, held it high above his head, then swiftly struck down, cutting one of the terrorist's heads clean off.

He passed the sword to me. "Want to have a go?"

I lifted the blade high, then down in a quick side movement, practiced so many times but never executed for real. Executed being the word. The head rolled three times, then stopped face down. Easier than I'd thought it would be. I dropped the sword and pulled out my knife. I sliced the remaining terrorists' ears off, stabbed out their eyes and slit their throats. Hey, if you've got a signature move, stick with it. The AC nodded. Time to go. Our job was done. Two lorries pulled up. We set the explosives they contained, and drove off. The compound would blow up. All the weapons would be destroyed. A lot of them came from China. Made me think.

We stopped 500 yards from the compound to watch our handiwork take hold. The blast lit up the sky for miles. We handed the observer, in his body bag, to the UN camp. It was war, real bullets. People died. No questions were asked. Our AC was a happy guy. We all got weekend passes. This looked like it might be fun. We needed it.

Next evening, we hit the city hard. Booze flowed. I watched as the guys got plastered, throwing money around. The bar was packed, plenty of loose women available for the right price. Then an announcer came onto the small stage, into the spotlight and spoke a few French words I understood. A woman floated on behind him, a microphone in her hand. She sang like an angel. Her voice filled the bar. She was beautiful. Dark skin, tall and slim, a tight-fitting white dress accentuating her figure. She oozed sex appeal. Stunning. Every guy in the bar watched her with hungry eyes, hard cocks, and their tongues hanging out. She sang for about thirty minutes, then disappeared backstage. The show was over for tonight.

Next mission: stop the weapons coming in. They mostly came across the border on mules, carried along the snarly mountain paths. I went with a group of 12 into the mountains. We'd been hiding there, camouflaged and watching, for three days and nights.

The days were oven-hot, the nights ice-cold. No campfires, no radio contact, no hot food. Day four, we caught a break. 12 noon, 300 yards away, we spotted a man, armed with a rifle, making his way slowly along the path. Fifty yards behind, the main convoy of mules and men. I counted ten men in total. Sniper rifle in hand, I waited until they were all out in the open. Then the corporal gave the order to fire.

I shot the guy at the back first. My fellow sniper, at the same time, got the guy at the front. Then all hell broke loose in a firefight that lasted only a few minutes but felt much, much longer. At the end, the ten terrorists lay dead. We made our way carefully down to the path. One bullet to each of their heads, just to be sure, and we shot the mules. Couldn't take them with us. Piled up all the weapons and ammo, threw in some explosives, found safe cover and detonated. The boom echoed around the mountains. Another day, more bloodshed, more deaths.

Chapter 22

That evening, I went to the club and watched the singer perform again, lust on my mind. When she finished her act, she came over and sat beside me. She spoke good English, with a French accent. A glass of bubbly was placed in front of her. We talked for a while, then she looked at me. "What do you want from me?" she asked, teasingly. "Please be honest." I liked her directness. No beating around the bush. "We're both adults," I said. "I think you know what I want." She downed her drink, stood up and said: "Let's go then. What are you waiting for?"

We went back to her place. It was a one-room home, in a block of run-down bedsits. Clean and tidy. She sat me down, then danced as she slowly undressed. Knelt down, naked, unzipped my trousers, held my cock in her hands. "I'll tell you what I want," she said. "A way out of this." She touched me with her tongue, using her lips to tease. Then started sucking, hard. My cock felt warm, her head bobbed up and down. I gritted my teeth and shot down her throat. She stood up, wiped her mouth, and, still naked, went to the kitchen area to make coffee.

She sat opposite me then, legs open. "Will you give me what I want?" she asked. I put down the untasted coffee, shook off my clothes and went over to her. I stood her up, bent her over the sofa and fucked her from behind. Grabbing a handful of her hair, I turned her face to me, slapped it three times, still pumping. I let go, reached under to her breasts, one nipple between each thumb and forefinger. I pinched hard, pulling and twisting, still pounding her from behind. She gasped in pain. I finished, coming hard. Standing over her, still inside her, I said: 'I'll give you what you want, whore. Now make some fresh coffee." She obeyed my command.

Next day, as agreed, I met her outside a 3-star hotel. She travelled light, one case. I booked her in, then we went up to her temporary new home. I paid the hotel manager in cash, gave her 10,000 US dollars. As agreed, she'd stay at the hotel until her travel papers were sorted. Then she'd go to France and a new life. She could bang out a song, maybe even reach some degree of stardom. Up to her. I just wanted a woman. It took the edge off the battle in my head. Sex, and lots of it, uncomplicated, no drama. Outside my daily duties, I spent all my time with her. She no longer worked at the club. We ate at the hotel restaurant, then up to her room for hard, cruel, uncomplicated sex.

One day, on daily patrol, the jeep in front hit a landmine. Blew ten feet into the air. We stopped sharp, rifles at the ready. Two guys already dead, the other two had their legs blown off and were screaming in agony. They were fucked. The medic injected them both with morphine. But if you're in the desert and your horse collapses, you shoot it, put it out of its misery. I looked at the Corporal. "I have to do this," I said. Pulled out my handgun and shot them both. I was breaking. The demons were all coming back, voices in my head, driving me insane. I took it all out on her. Beat her black and blue, bit her, flogged her, fucked her hard up her tight virgin arse. I wanted someone else to feel my pain, my anger. I was deranged. Afterwards, I collapsed on top of her, shut my eyes. She was crying. What had I done to her? Why? Fuck. What was wrong with me? "I'm sorry," I heard myself whisper. "I'm so sorry. So sorry."

When the announcement came, I think all the guys breathed a sigh of relief. We sat in the mess room, listened to the radio. The war was over. Party time, all over the country. Happy people dancing in the streets. We became watchmen, checking people in and out of the new French embassy. Searching anyone suspicious for weapons. I was glad the war was over, but this was dull. I wanted out. Time for a change. Get back on track.

A week later, I was on the main gate, bored and restless. Marianne appeared. I'd told her to come today. I was going to get her fast-tracked. She looked at me, smiled. I walked her into the embassy and pointed her towards the office, where she'd register, then went back to my post. A couple of hours later, there she was, walking towards me, all smiles. "See you tonight," she said, and winked. I smiled and patted her bum.

Four months later, I got her papers. I'd spoken to an official at the embassy, bribed him a little. Alright, bribed him a lot. I spoke to an Italian guy, one of my fellow legionnaires. He had connections in France. He wrote down the name and address of a club. That evening I gave her the papers, along with the extra info.

She was booked on the morning flight to Paris, then on to Marseilles. I gave her a bag of cash. "Please do it hard tonight," I said. I took my clothes off and lay face down on the bed. She picked up a bamboo cane and beat me hard for 20 minutes, then took her dress off and lay down beside me, wrapping her arms around my body. I shut my eyes and slept. Next morning. I took her to the airport. If she didn't make it as a singer, she could make it as a porn star. She was my kind of woman.

I still had close to three years to do in the Legion. We were locked in at the embassy 24/7. Twelve hours on duty, twelve hours off. A handful of extremists still wanted us out, completely out. About a month after Marianne's departure, two of us were on gate duty, watching for suicide bombers. I heard a shot. It hit the wall by my head. "Down, down!" I screamed. "Sniper!" Too late. When a high-velocity bullet hits a human skull, you don't need a doctor. Half his head was splattered on the ground. Shots were fired by our own marksmen from the roof of the embassy, the sniper was long gone. Back to tell his mates how brave he was.

It was my birthday. I was 26 years old. Once again, happy fucking birthday to me. No cake today.

The incident, in the end, it got me what I wanted — out. When his personal belongs were bagged up, his phone was scrutinised. Big problem. The prick had filmed me and the AC beheading the terrorists. We were frog-marched into the General's office. He played it for us three fucking times. We'd been stupid. Eyes wide open at all times. Fuck.

He threw the phone at me. "Destroy that," he barked. "If that ever got out, we'd be disbanded. What the fuck were you thinking?"

I shrugged. "It was war," was all I said.

We'd get a discharge, back to France. No-one would ever find out. Our papers would state discharge on medical grounds. Instant citizenship. Interesting.

We packed our bags and were escorted to the airport. A night flight back to France and Legion HQ in Paris. After, we went for coffee. "What are you going to do now?" he asked. Big question. He had plans of his own. He'd sell his services to the highest bidder, become a mercenary. As he stood to leave, he wrote his name and phone number on our café bill. I wished him good luck and watched him go. I stuck the bill inside my book.

I bought some new clothes, booked into a hotel. Took a long hot bath. Came out, got dressed and found a note slipped under my door. I headed down to the hotel restaurant. There she was, dressed to impress. I smiled, sat down and said "Good to see you." She smiled. "Ditto," she said. Then she started laughing. "The French Foreign Legion?" she giggled. "What the fuck were you thinking?"

"I was bored," I said. "I needed a break."

We went up to my room. Had she been sent to kill me? I'd let her, no problem. She locked the door, turned to face me. Stepped out of her dress. "Fuck me," she said. "Fuck me hard." She was my wife so I willingly obliged.

Later, dressed in bathrobes and sipping strong French coffee, we sat and talked. We never mentioned her dead brother. She hadn't been sent to kill me. She'd been sent to offer a new deal. Her uncle was in great danger, enemies closing in fast. He urgently needed my skills. He'd closed the brothels.

He'd closed the Candy Man shops. My fucking shops. I was amazed to find myself so angry.

Ling flicked her laptop on, showed me a Swiss bank account number with five million US Dollars inside. It was in my name. To be honest, I'd have taken the deal for free. I'd have done it to keep my wife alive.

⎯⎯⎯⎯⎯⎯⎯⎯ • ⎯⎯⎯⎯⎯⎯⎯⎯

Chapter 23

London. Back at the flat, Ling handed me a small holdall. I opened it, put on the dual shoulder holster, loaded the two guns and put my jacket back over them. The Candy Man was back in business.

We met Ling's uncle at the restaurant. He was a worried old man. The gang war was way out of control, police all over everyone. Arrests had been made. Business was declining. The Russians and Albanians had formed an alliance. Together, they had the firepower and the men to destroy us. This had to be broken, put to bed. Fast. I wrote a long list of stuff we'd need and handed it to him. The weapons turned up, three days later.

Our first target was the new Russian gang boss. Start at the top and filter down. I lay on a rooftop overlooking their main office, sheltered by a minicab firm.

Six guys came out, looked up and down the road. Then the boss walked onto the pavement, heading for his car. Breathing slow, I aimed and fired. He was dead before he hit the tarmac. The bodyguards drew their weapons, but, without a visible target, they just ran around like the proverbial headless chickens.

I stood up, a heavy machine gun in my hands. I rained bullets, ripped them to pieces. Emptied the whole magazine. Ling, at close range, finished the job. She dropped a small bag into the car and two bags of candy on the bloodied pavement. Phase one, complete.

I made my way to our rendezvous point, picked up Ling, looked back and pressed the detonator button. The explosion rocked the car as we drove away. Ling expertly reloaded our weapons as we headed for phase two.

We both jumped out at the Albanian headquarters, guns blazing. Two submachine guns at close range sort most problems out. Again, two bags of candy on the pavement as we left. Again,

I pressed the remote. A huge boom. No idea how many dead. Numbers, just numbers.

Next day, front page news: Candy Man Strikes Again. Just the start. The first message. Don't ever fuck with us.

Night after night for a month we hit hard. We waited for them to hit back. Nothing. The war had gone on too long. It disrupted business. It cost money. In the end, peace talks were urgently called.

We chose the venue. A small warehouse in the east end. The gangs rolled up. As hosts, it was our duty to keep the area secure. We'd called all our men back to London for a show of strength. We let each gang boss in with two bodyguards. No weapons. Ling's uncle sat at the head of the table. The map of London was redrawn. Everyone knew exactly where they could do business, exactly where their boundaries were. War is war, but business is business.

The Candy Man shops would reopen as a kind of franchise. We'd keep opening all over the UK, dealing with local gangs as we grew. We'd pay them a grand a week for every shop. A simple plan — my idea. I still wanted a shop in every town, this was the way to get there. The profits would more than outweigh the loss.

Meeting over, we took the afternoon off. Back to the flat. Ling had sorted out the damage caused my Zen's bomb — it was mostly to the entranceway. The steel door had taken the worst of the blast. She looked happy, bashing around in the small kitchen. I went down to the backyard, hung up my punch bag and worked out for a couple of hours. A quiet dinner together, talking. Like a normal couple. A normal life. Ling asked me what I wanted. That was a deep question to ask me. Easy to answer. I fetched my book and showed her. I told her what my dad did. Run away.

All the old photos, the drawing I'd done when I was a boy. My dad on his knees, sword through his chest. I'd added to the drawing, over the years. More blood. More flames. More fury. Fucking hated him.

Ling had tears rolling down her face, holding my hand. "Trust me, James," she said. "I'll never run away from you. I'll never leave you."

The following night, at dinner with her uncle, we spoke about the business. He wanted me to be more involved, his right-hand man. I knew what he was thinking. I knew too much. I might become a threat. So move me up the ladder, give me a reason protect their business. The boss of two nightclubs and a casino, used to launder the drug money, as well as the Candy Man expansion programme. I smiled. I was back on track.

Takings were down at the casino. Someone had been stealing. It was my call how to deal with it. There was a lot of money involved, astonishing really. A sign of how bad things had become. I believed lack of leadership was to blame. That evening, twenty minutes before opening, I introduced myself to my staff. Ling and six guys by my side.

We went up to the manager's office. He sat down, sweat on his brow. He was responsible and accountable for the casino. So, in my mind, he was responsible and accountable for the missing cash. "Takings are down," I said. "Tell me why." He babbled a bit about the economic climate, fewer guests, a load of bollocks. Too much cash was missing. I stopped him. "We can do one of two things," I said. "One, I can shoot you right now. Two, you can pay back the missing cash." He chose neither, still babbling, still protesting innocence. Wasting my valuable time.

The office door swung open. His wife, escorted by two of my bodyguards, came in. Her hands were tied behind her back. He stood up, still pleading with me. I hit him, hard, and he dropped to the floor. I pulled him up, sat him on a chair, tied him up. His mouth was gagged with tape. No more babbling. I had his full attention. His wife was also tied to a chair and positioned opposite her husband. My two assistants rolled out polythene, covering the plush carpet. They were wheeled onto the temporary cover. I looked at Ling and smiled.

We called in the assistant manager. I gave him my card. He saw the Candy Man logo, kept silent. "Tonight my friends, we're going to play a game," I said. "It's called 'some you win, some you lose'."

First I shaved the managers head, then his wife's. Picked up my flick knife, roughly cut all their clothes off. A little bit for show, a little bit to save time later. She was a pretty fit-looking woman. Shame Ling was there, could have had a gang bang with her husband watching on. Never mind. I screwed the silencer onto my gun.

Slipped the safety off, shot the woman in her knee, then did the same to her husband. "Where's the money?" I asked, pulling the tape from his mouth. "I've not stolen any money," he gasped. "Please, please believe me!"

I shook my head, tape back on his lying mouth. Shot out his other knee, then ditto his wife. Still nothing.

I was wasting time. I sighed, took off my jacket. Then my shoulder holster, shirt, shoes, socks, trousers. I stood before my audience in my trunks. Almost like the old boxing days, really. I picked up my old flick knife. In a well-practiced move, I sliced both his ears off, then stabbed out his eyes. Pent-up rage took over. I kept stabbing, again and again. Don't know how many times. Then, suddenly, I turned to the assistant manager, pulled him onto the cover. "Where's the money?" I rasped. No answer. Just a wide-eyed stare.

Elbow strike to the face, knife up under the ribcage, straight to the heart. Fuck the money. No-one would ever steal from me again after this. I stepped off the polythene. "Get me a fucking towel," I snapped. One appeared. I wiped the blood off my body, got dressed. "Clean this mess up," I said, walking towards the door, then I hear a voice asking, "What about the woman?" What a stupid question. I shook my head.

Fuck's sake. Did I have to do everything myself? Could they not think? I turned back, pulled my gun, stared at the woman, for a couple of seconds. Shot her six times in her shaved head, point blank. I walked down the stairs and stood by the rather large roulette wheel. "Give me 10k worth of chips" I said to the croupier. I placed the lot on black. Watched the hypnotic wheel spin. The tiny steel ball bounced into a red slot. Game over for tonight.

Chapter 24

We went home. I went to our bedroom, stripped off. "Do it," I told Ling. "Do it now, fucking hard." I lay face down on the bed. She got the 18-inch leather flogger and beat me, hard, for 20 minutes. I wanted her to beat the devil out of me. When she stopped I got up without a word, went into the bathroom, turned the shower on. I stayed in there for ages, trying to wash the blood and the anger away. I sat down, water still running, and closed my eyes. It was all starting again. The shops, the drugs, the constant violence. The blood. So much blood. The rage inside. Not good.

As a kid, I'd dreamed of a peaceful life. The closest I'd ever come was that honeymoon with Ling in the cabin on the mountain. That was what I really wanted. So why could I never seem to get there? What kept pulling me back? What made me this evil monster I'd clearly become? "Take me back," I said, over and over again. "Take me back." No. No going back for the Candy Man. More of the same stretched ahead. Work, work, work. Death, death, death. Enough. Time to get out for good. If I carried on, I'd end up like her dad. An evil, ruthless man. No way. Not me.

I managed to get up, turn the shower off, dry my battered skin. I went quietly to our bedroom, where Ling lay asleep. Picked up my shoulder holster, went into the lounge. The moon shone brightly through the window. I drew a gun. Flicked the safety off. Put it under my chin, pointed upwards. I'd had enough. Time to leave. I saw a silhouette appear in the doorway, and smiled as I pulled the trigger. A click, nothing more. I squeezed again. A click. The gun was empty. Just like me. I'd lost the plot. Fucked up again.

Ling took it from my shaking hand, helped me to stand and took me to the bedroom. "You're tired, my love," she soothed. "Sleep, beloved husband. Sleep now." I listened to her breathing, felt her gentle hand on my heart. It was so quiet, so calm. I felt like she was keeping my heart beating, if only just. We stayed that way all night.

She was gone the next morning when I woke. I got up, looked for my guns. Also gone. She must have taken them with her. I went back to bed and shut my eyes, fighting the images of all the people I'd killed. Ghosts. They kept coming at me. Nothing I could do. I'd made each choice. Guilty as sin. I'd created my own bed of nails and I was trapped on it.

"All because of him," I kept thinking. "All because of him."

I heard the door open and close. Ling came back and sat on the bed. "James," she said, "you're not well. I'm here. I'm going to help you heal."

Two days later, she guided me onto the family jet, on our way to China. We went straight to the cabin on the mountain. I slept for two days and nights, safe and away from the world. Ling stayed glued to my side. Two weeks of unbroken peace, of just being a normal couple, with a normal life. I was calm, the ghosts gone for now. The little voice in my head stilled. This was not a time for me to go mental.

Week three, with Christmas approaching, we came down the mountain to stay with Ling's Mum. We started training again, going through the graceful but deadly moves for two hours each day. Slowly getting back into some kind of routine. Slowly clearing my mind. We'd have a family Christmas celebration, then fly back to London.

Christmas day, we sat at the grand dining table. Lisa, my beloved sister, was guest of honour. It was so good to see her. She was so beautiful, clearly so happy with her life in China. It was a wonderful time, a family time. When we got back to London, I felt ready to hit the ground running.

Back at the flat, Ling handed me my guns. I'd made her a promise. She knew I wouldn't try to kill myself again. I thanked her, put the shoulder holster on, guns loaded and ready. She went off to see her uncle, catch up on business. I'd meet her later at the restaurant. I had my own keep to earn.

I went to the clubs first, spoke to the managers about the improvements I wanted before New Year's Eve, our biggest night of the year. Topless waitresses, tight red bikini bottoms, pushing booze and drugs to the customers. Half price drinks all night. Top DJs with big followings. They agreed. Well, they had no fucking choice.

I picked up the cash takings, headed to the casino to meet the new manager, make sure he knew his place in the hierarchy and what had happened to his predecessor. Picked up his takings. Then round the shops. As I put the last three bags of cash on the back seat, I noticed the rear suspension. Rock bottom. Clearly, this hadn't been done in a while. This was a bad joke. I wasn't laughing.

"Go steady," I told the driver. We didn't have far to travel, we should be okay. A deep pothole had other ideas. The suspension collapsed. Fucking great. Now I'd have to wait for new cars, new drivers. Half an hour of my time later, with my temper back to boiling point, two new Mercs pulled up. We shifted the bags and took off for the restaurant. Twenty minutes later, I strode up to the table, where Ling sat beside her uncle. "Why didn't anyone collect the cash while we were away?" I said, voice level. He shrugged his shoulders. "Your job," he replied, not even looking up.

I stared at him. Old fool. All that cash lying around. All that temptation. He'd made us a prime target for thievery, from our own people or anyone else stupid enough to try it. He'd shown total lack of responsibility, left us vulnerable. Everything we'd sorted before leaving for China, left hanging out to dry. Weak. Stupid. Arrogant. Lazy.

I threw a small bag of candy on the table, shook my head, drew a gun and shot him, just once, middle of the forehead. The force jolted him backwards. He slid to the tiled marble floor. Ripping the tasteless gold chain and medallion from his lifeless neck, I dumped it on the table in front of Ling.

"She's the boss now," I said to the bodyguards, who hadn't moved a muscle. "Look after her better than you looked after this old fool. Now clean this mess the fuck up and someone get me a coffee."

They moved off. Ling looked at me. "Why?" was all she said. "We need a strong leader," I said. "He was weak. He put our business in jeopardy. Could have lost us everything we've built. You're strong, you command respect. Take control."

The word went out on the street. Ling was the new boss. Keep things simple. Less drama.

Chapter 25

I had big plans for January and Ling would be very busy.

I'd been to see the manager of one of our clubs, a cabaret joint with comedians, singers, strippers and so on. Given him the name of a real class act. Two weeks later, he called. My performer was in town. He'd booked her into a top-class hotel, allocated her a car and driver for the duration of her stay. Full five-star treatment. She had a one-hour slot booked each night, and this week I was going to make sure she earned her pay.

I watched her perform that first night. She had talent, for sure. The audience loved her. Standing ovation. After her set, at my request, she was escorted to the office. As she entered, I greeted her with open arms. After a quick hug, I locked the door.

Marianne looked hot. It had been a long time since she boarded a plane to Paris.

We didn't speak. I simply went over, unzipped her dress. It slithered to the floor. She had no underwear on. Men would die right now to be in my shoes. I eased her to her knees, unzipped my trousers. Looking up with a wry smile, she bent forward. Her magical tongue and lips hadn't lost their touch. I could feel myself throbbing, had to have her. I stood her up, moved her over to the desk and bent her over. Rammed into her, deep as I could go. Paused for a moment, savouring her hot, tight wetness. God, I'd missed her. Slowly, I started moving, back and forth, back and forth. Her tight little arse ground into me, she was whimpering, groaning, clutching the sides of the desk. Faster and faster, lost to everything but this intense, red, shuddering moment. Grabbing her hair, pulling hard, I thrust one last time, teeth gritted, pinning her to the desk as I came.

I pulled out, turned her over, then pointed at the Nespresso machine in the corner. "Coffee for two, my dear." The first words either of us had spoken.

Actually, there was no need for words. I undressed. We sipped our coffee in silence. Then I got up and bent over the desk. She picked up the bamboo cane from its stand beside the door and beat me, hard, for about ten minutes. I straightened up, pulled her to me, we kissed. Passionately, violently. I picked up a cushion from the couch, placed it against her head, and hit her with a right hook. She sank back to her knees. Grabbing her hair, I pulled her head back, shoved my cock deep into her throat. She didn't even blink, just started sucking, like it was the only thing she'd ever wanted to do.

Later, as she left, I said: "Good to see you, whore. Same time tomorrow." She breezed away, never a backwards glance, never a word of complaint. She was truly my whore. She took it all in her stride. For a week, we followed more or less the same ritual. Barely speaking, just raging, violent, painful, wonderful sex. It was a special connection.

Every night, I went home a happy guy. Showered and went to bed with my wife. Even when Marianne's gig was up and she went back to Paris, the memories kept me going. Business was good, things were ticking over like clockwork. Time for another little break. Our second in command was a loyal man, we could trust him to look after things. And besides, there was something I really wanted to do.

We flew to Spain. Geoff and his missus, Vera, met us at the airport. I was so fucking happy to see him. In his way, he was the foundation for all of it. The first one to give me a chance. The man who set me on the path to wealth, power, status, strength. Even my beautiful wife was, in part, thanks to him. Geoff was one of the good guys.

After introductions, Geoff drove us to their little slice of paradise, the villa they'd retired to so long ago. We sat on the patio, in the sun, cold drinks before us. While Vera gave Ling the guided tour, I took in the surroundings. Bit grubby. Paintwork peeling. Some cracked tiles on the patio, weeds growing through. Even the glasses in front of us were chipped. I asked Geoff how life was treating him. He broke down and told me the lot.

He was running out of money, and had stupidly started gambling. The debt was significant, and the bookies wanted their money. Big problem for Geoff. Not a problem for me. "You should have come to me, Geoff," I said. "I'm your friend. You helped me out, why wouldn't you ask me to help you?"

I already knew the answer. Pride, at first, then shame. I didn't need him to say it. I held up a hand. "It's okay, Geoff," I said. "Let's just get this sorted." I pulled out my laptop, opened that Swiss bank account Ling had set up — it was already a much larger bank account than it had been, and it had been pretty freaking huge to begin with. Geoff gave me his details. I transferred €1.5million to his account. He stared at me.

"That'll pay the debts, get this place done up," I said. "Get you somewhere else, if you want. And give you enough to live on for the rest of your life." He opened his mouth. "No argument," I said. "And no thanks. Just a promise: no more gambling." He took my hand and shook it, nodding, eyes spilling. I clapped his shoulder, turned away to give him a moment. Geoff's pride was rock hard. My debt was paid and his problems were solved. All even.

We spent a fortnight in Spain, like any other couple. Took Geoff and Vera out and about, even got to see the contractors arrive to start fixing things up. Geoff — or more likely Vera — wasn't going to hang about when there were no more obstacles in the way. They were happy. It made me happy, too. Like maybe some sort of Karmic balance had been restored. Maybe. I liked the old guy. Geoff reminded me of my grandpa.

Meantime, Ling and I had the chance to enjoy one another again. Talking, laughing, lots of sex. Not the hard, cold, brutal sex I enjoyed so much with Marianne. This was fiery and passionate, there was tenderness too. Plenty of lust, a little dusting of love. I didn't feel guilty about my liaisons with Marianne. They had nothing to do with my life with Ling. They were just another way to vent the violence that never seemed far away. I didn't want to hurt my wife. I wanted to protect and care for her. She was part of me in a way Marianne, or any other woman for that matter, could never be. And for that I owed her a debt, too. This was the life I wanted. Having fun.

Ling's birthday was at the end of our fortnight. I'd planned a surprise. "We're going to Monte Carlo," I announced, as we boarded our jet. She raised an eyebrow, nodded, beamed a smile at me. The woman trusted me. We landed safely, went straight to the Port Palace hotel. Our suite's French windows led to a balcony looking over the marina. "Look at that beauty," I said, pointing to a brand-new Sunseeker 131 sparkling in the sun. "Gorgeous, isn't she?" Ling nodded, sighed. "It's beautiful here," she said. "I could get used to it."

"Come on," I said. "Let's go for a walk."

We headed down to the docks, straight towards the Sunseeker. Ling stopped, a surprised gasp on her lips. The yacht's name was Ling. "Happy birthday, my love," I said, handing over the keys. It was a special moment shared.

●

Chapter 26

A week later, I was in Vegas. First time in the States. I was meeting with a Columbian drug boss, arranging a long-term deal for supplies of top-notch Cocaine. Business went well. I was on a high. I got back to my hotel room. Time for some fun. I showered quick, got dressed to impress and headed for the bright lights. I was on an early morning flight next day, the night was young, so was I. Not into gambling — never had been — I chose a high-class strip club. Twenty minutes in, not unexpected, a woman sat down next to me. "How are you tonight?" she asked, hand on my thigh. "Want some company?" I answered with my dick, not my head. "Sure," I said. "Let me buy you a drink."

Her name — or the name she gave me — was Julie Brown. 24 years old, shoulder length blond hair, five-eight, California tan and Colgate smile. High tits, great ass. We chatted for a bit, for form's sake, then went back to my hotel. Four hours of energetic fucking later, I nodded off. I'd set my alarm for 5.30am. Plenty of time to get to the airport.

I slept a deep, untroubled sleep, woke at 6.30am. She'd turned the alarm off so we could sleep. Fury rose, she quickly apologized, got up, moving at lightning speed. "Hit the shower," she said. "I'll pack your stuff and get you a cab." 15 minutes later, I checked out and jumped into the waiting cab. Still time to make the flight. I thanked Julie and handed her a wad of clean bills. She'd earned them. Good fun, no drama.

I ended up with an hour or so before boarding, so I went and had breakfast and a much-needed coffee. Suddenly felt uneasy. You know, the feeling you get when something's not right. I should have legged it there and then. Hindsight is a wonderful thing. A sniffer dog approached, apparently very excited by my hand luggage.

Bollocks. I was surrounded by armed officers, and taken to an interrogation room.

Not a good start to the day.

In handcuffs, I watched as my bag was placed on the table, then emptied of its contents. Fuck. Out pops, like a rabbit from a top hat, a large bag of white powder. I'd been well and truly set up by the luscious Julie. I'd been a fool. I was so angry with myself. I'd forgotten my number one rule: trust no-one.

I was taken to a courthouse, put in front of a judge. No bail. Straight to a high-security prison in the desert, awaiting trial. I used my one call to phone Ling. I told her I'd been set up, not about Julie. Ling was going to call Lisa in her capacity as our family lawyer. She'd fly in from China.

Lisa visited, went through the case notes. Not much she could do, I'd been caught red-handed with 2 kilos of cocaine. She said my best bet was to plead guilty, go for the minimum first-offence term. I was 27 years old and facing five years in a US prison. If I behaved, I might be out in three. What a fucking mess.

It went down like Lisa said. Five years, bang. Back to the desert fun house. My only plan was to keep my head down, do my time, get out as quickly as possible. I'd pass all the time I could training in my cell. I had nothing better to do. After about a week, I was spotted by an eagle-eyed guard and taken to see the warden.

He sat me down and offered me the chance of my own cell, with a shower. Good food and special privileges, like access to the guards' gym. All I had to do was get in on his fighting ring.

Basically, it was bare-knuckle boxing. No rules, no referee, anything goes. Last man standing takes the prize. He thought it was much-needed entertainment. I thought he was fucking mad. It would give me something to focus on, stop me going crazy. Plus, it was a little like going back to my youth, to the boxing and martial arts clubs I'd loved so much. "Give me a week to get ready," I said.

I wanted to witness some fights first hand. Saw three. Beyond brutal. Like Roman gladiators, without weapons. Two guys got locked in the fight cage, one came out a winner. One guy was beaten to death. The other two losers, barely alive, were dragged unceremoniously from the blood-spattered cage.

My first fight was arranged. My opponent was a big Italian guy. I'd seen him train. A heavyweight. Unbeaten. This was serious stuff. The warden had offered me some words of encouragement. "I've got a lot riding on you," he'd said. "Don't fucking lose."

Trust me, I had no intention of losing. I stepped into that cage angry, ready for war. A bell sounded. He came at me like a mad bull. With 20 fights behind him, he was a dangerous man. Tonight, though, he was going down. I'd break most of his bones. Then I'd kill him. I didn't want a rematch.

I ducked his wild punches. Then hit him hard in the ribcage, 1-2-3. My fists, hardened from years of training, were too much for his bones. I heard the snaps, saw the grimace of pain. He slowed down, trying to think. No point. I had something to prove. Had to put on a show of strength, had to make them all remember me. Two swift kicks to the groin, a fast, hard, low sidekick to his left knee. He threw another haymaker. I grabbed his wrist, twisted his arm, smashed my fist down on his elbow. Stepped back and kicked him, just under the shoulder. One broken arm, one dislocated collarbone. Oh, and one damaged knee, which gave way. He went down. I moved in fast and rained punches to his face.

The Italian guy tried to grab hold. I slipped behind him, hit him with a sledgehammer blow to the upper spine. He screamed — fracture. I paused a few seconds, stalking him, ready for the kill. He was a low punch bag. Time for a good workout. Kick, kick, kick, to his head. He flopped over, face down on the blood-soaked concrete floor. I pinned him down, one knee on his back. I punched his ribcage with both fists, right behind his heart. Bones cracked, one after the other.

I was sweating. I pulled his lifeless head up, by the ears, bashed it down hard, again and again. Lifted it one last time and rammed a Karate chop to his neck. He was already dead, the show of power had to go on. I held his head in both hands, pulled it fast to the left, then to the right. I think everyone must have heard the crackle, the place was almost silent. I turned him over, sat on his chest and kept punching his face, harder and harder. I didn't hear the cage door open. Four guards grabbed me, pulled me off, still swinging. The fight was over. I'd won this battle.

I stood up, covered in blood, and raised my arms high. No cheers or applause. Silence, not a sound. Fine. I went willingly back to my cell, took a shower. Time to switch off.

I'd done what I had to do, no more, no less. I was alive. I slept a deep, untroubled sleep. In the morning, bright and early, a very happy Warden brought me breakfast himself. Steak, eggs, bacon, tomatoes, hash browns. "Hell, boy," he said, in a deep Southern Carolina accent. "That was some kinda fight. I'm gonna like having you around." He dropped 500 dollars on my bunk and went on his way. Later I was taken to the gym hall, where I trained for three hours. No one spoke to me. I stayed focused, in a world of my own. I'd make it. I'd pass this test.

If you're going through hell, keep going.

●

Chapter 27

Prison life turned out not to be so bad. I used my time to great advantage. I read books, trained hard. Fought. Repeat. I kept up my training in my special skills, too — Dim Mak, the death touch, taught to me what seemed like a lifetime ago, by a Grand Master in China. I practiced those moves, at night, in my cell, well out of sight. I'd never used them. They were a last resort.

I fought anyone stupid enough to get in the cage with me. Beat almost all of them to death. Some I allowed to survive, those who wouldn't pose a threat to me afterwards. Rookies, mostly. Boys who didn't know better, who still had a chance to learn. The rest, no. Their lives were over the second they volunteered to fight me.

I was allowed to phone Ling once a week. Without me to keep things moving in London, the business had collapsed. She hadn't been able to get the other Triads on side. They saw our deal with the other gangs as a betrayal. We should have approached them first. So, outnumbered, she'd sounded the retreat, moved back to China.

I sent her a lot of visiting cards. I knew it was difficult for her to travel, she was running the Chinese side of the business on her own. She came when she could.

A guard opened my cell door. "You have a visitor, inmate," he said. They didn't bark at me like they did the others. They'd seen me fight. I saw the fear in their eyes.

I followed the guard to the visiting area. I sat down on one side of the inch-thick reinforced security glass, picked up the phone. "Hello James," she smiled. "How are you?" Even now, after everything, Ling was mine, my woman, my wife for better or worse. The only person on the planet I trusted with my life. She loved me, with all her heart. I missed her. I missed women. Smooth skin, gentle curves, soft, hot wetness. Fuck. Like she could read my mind, Ling opened her coat, just enough to show me her naked breasts. She wasn't wearing anything else. Just for me.

She looked different. I couldn't put my finger on why. Fuck it, it had been almost three years. I probably looked really different too. "I love you, James," she said, as she got up to leave. "I do love you." I played the words over and over again in my mind. I couldn't wait to be free, to be with her again.

It was, thank fuck, countdown time. My release was in three days. Tonight was my final fight. The arena was packed to the rafters, the atmosphere electric. My opponent had been brought in from another prison. He was a notorious Russian, a killer, a giant of a man at six foot four and 18 stone. The odds were heavily against me, no-one except the big guys would agree to fight me now. My only chance was to finish things fast. I had a plan, simple tonight. Ding fucking ding. The crowd roared. He came steaming in hard, he was too big to be fast. I ducked and dodged. No time for a performance tonight, no fucking about.

Last resort.

I hit him three hard blows, right over the heart. He dropped like a sack of coal. The fight was over before it started. He was dead before his head bounced off the concrete. I stood by the exit door and waited.

Silence. The guard who opened the cage door stood back, well out of my way. I walked back to my cell alone. For once, no blood on me. I still spent ages in the shower. Some stains you can't remove.

Next day, the warden came to my cell. No cheery Southern banter this time. He just dropped $500 on the bunk, shook his head and walked away. He was scared of me. They all were. No matter. In two more days, I'd be free.

Another birthday. 30 years old. And what a gift. Freedom. After three brutal years in this madhouse, it was time to leave. The warden did me one last favour, and released me at 6am. If he'd waited until 2pm, the usual time, the cops would have been waiting to deport me back to the UK. Instead, I could take care of one little thing in Vegas, then go straight to the airport, fly to China and surprise my wife, my family.

The guard opened the electric gate and wished me good luck. "What are you going to do now?" he asked.

I smiled as I stepped through, a free man. "Anything I want," I replied. "Anything I fucking want."

Chapter 28

I started walking. Nothing to see but desert and a long road. I never looked back. Forget what lies behind, the best is yet to come. I walked towards my true destiny. It was hot, I was already sweating. I was alive. A happy guy. After about half an hour, a beat-up old Ford came along. I hitched from the kind old couple inside. Made it back to Vegas. Checked into a hotel, made some calls. Then ran a hot bath. I lay back and relaxed for the first time in three years.

One room service dinner later, steak and fries with all the trimmings, it was time for sleep. I woke in time for a spectacular sunrise. A new dawn and a new life.

The hotel was ok. I sat on the balcony, overlooking Vegas and eating a breakfast of pancakes. I had all the time in the world. Later, I wandered around the shops, bought some new clothes and shoes. Had lunch at a café, watching the people go by. That evening, suited and booted, I went to a strip club. A bored-looking waitress in a skimpy bikini top and hot pants took my order. Sparkling mineral water. She shrugged and wandered off.

The show started. A spotlight hit the small stage. A woman appeared, danced while removing her clothes. She was still attractive, still had a firm body, nice tits. I stared at her. Fucking cock sucking bitch. She finished her crappy act. I left my drink unfinished, went round to the back of the building. She came out five minutes later, lit a fag.

"Hello, Julie," I said, stepping out of the shadows and punching her in the stomach. I closed the door as I pulled her into the darkness. I hit her again. "Who paid you to set me up?" No answer was the wrong answer. I pulled her up, slapped her twice. "Who paid you?" I said. Calm. No emotion. No answer.

I held the knife to her face. Fear in her eyes. Now she remembered. "One more chance, Julie," I said. "Tell me who set me up."

"Some woman," she gasped. "I met some woman at the club. She paid me. $10,000. She paid me to set you up." I nodded, asked her to describe the woman. A shiver ran down my spine as she reeled off the basics. Her? Why the fuck would she do that to me? It didn't make any sense.

I helped the stripper to stand, thanked her for the information. Then I broke her neck and dropped her with the trash. Dirty fucking bitch. Stitch me up, you fucking die.

I went back to the hotel. Time to leave the USA. No trip to China now. I packed my bags, made some calls, then phoned Ling. I had a new plan. A quick buying trip to a specialist sports shop.

Chapter 29

Ihitched a bumpy ride across the border in the back of a lorry. No papers, expired passport. No-one searched the lorries or cars going into Mexico. It was all one-way traffic, so many Mexicans trying to get to the land of the free. I gave the lorry driver $1,000 for his trouble. He dropped me at a train station. As the train pulled away, I shut my eyes and nodded off to sleep. A long journey lay ahead.

It took me a week to get to Mexico City. Fucking trains were a nightmare. I got a cab to a 4-star hotel, close to a gym. I'd be spending a lot of time there. It was okay, clean and tidy. I paid six months up front, dumped my bag and headed across the road to a seedy-looking bar. Tipping the barman $100 for my dirty glass of flat mineral water, I asked him who to see about new papers. He pointed a grubby finger to a guy at the end of the beer-stained bar. I walked over and sat next to him. He stank. "I need some help," I said.

I wanted a new UK passport and driving license, a new identity. I gave him my old passport and my new name, along with $500 up front. He'd get the rest when the job was done.

My new name was James Black, Jimmy (Boy) Black. A world middleweight boxing champion in waiting. This was a vital step towards my revenge. I went back to the hotel, phoned my wife. Went out on the balcony, clenched my fists, stared at my knuckles, hardened like steel by years of punching, breaking boards, blocks, and bones. They were my gift, and I'd use them to their full potential. I had lightning speed and frightening power. Hit harder than a heavyweight and was as fast as a flyweight. A magical combination.

This wasn't a new career. It was an obsession. I was a machine, hell-bent on revenge. Revenge for a life I'd never get to have. Revenge for three wasted years. Money wasn't the object, I had millions stashed away. More than enough to forget it all, retire and live a good life with Ling. No. My war would never be over, not while I had breath. I might have made a lot of bad moves. I was still in the game. I could still get to the top. Nothing was going to stop me.

No time to waste. I jogged to the crummy gym. As I pushed the old wooden door, I imagined all the hungry fighters, who had walked this path before. This gym, crappy and stinking as it was, had produced some legends of the ring. And I was going to be next one.

My plan was simple. I'd fight out of Mexico for a year. Get myself noticed as a professional boxer. Then move to Detroit, USA. Become World Champion, then retire. I glanced around the old gym, walked over to the small office. "No gringos," said one of the old guys inside. "Guys, that's racist," I said. He just looked at me, dully. "No gringos," he said again.

"How about a test," I said. "I'll go up against your best fighter right now. If I win, you let me train here. If I lose, I'll pay you one thousand US Dollars." Money speaks, and it speaks loud. He grunted, and jerked a thumb at the changing rooms. I picked up my bag and walked in. Fuck, the smell — old sweat and piss from the broken toilets. An old guy walked in, threw a pair of old sparring gloves on the broken tiled floor. I tied my new, soft leather boots, picked up my new gloves. Kicked the old pair out of my way.

My opponent was already in the ring. I jumped, smiled, nodded, put my mouth guard in. Everyone had stopped to watch this beat-up-looking old gringo get what was coming to him. A good show of power was needed. The bell went. Time to switch it on. He came at me, threw a couple of left jabs, a right hook.

I bobbed and weaved, easily avoiding the blows. I moved in with a 1-2-3 to his stomach and ribs, then a right hook to his jaw and two left hooks to the side of his head. He was out like a light. Jaws had dropped open all around the ring. Turned out, he was the official Mexican Middleweight Champion.

I took my gloves off, stepped out of the ring, took out my mouth guard. "When do I start?" I asked.

Chapter 30

I fought all over Mexico for a year. 22 hard fights, all knockouts. Unbeaten. The fans chanted my name: Ice Gringo, Ice gringo, Ice gringo. My contract was up and it was time to move on.

I went to the US embassy for a visa. All my forged papers passed official scrutiny. Two days later, visa in my back pocket, I was on my way to the airport in Mexico City. Ling met me there. "Alright," she said, after we'd exchanged long hugs. "Talk me through this again. You don't need the money. So why boxing, James? Why the fuck are you boxing?"

I explained the whole plan. It was the only way I could see to get my revenge, to find peace, to be able to retire to a life with her in China. Maybe, with luck, another two years would do it. Then it would all be over. We'd be together for the rest of our lives.

She agreed to fly me to Detroit. We used the flight time well. By the time we hit tarmac at Detroit Metro, we both had new memberships to the mile-high club. Ling wasn't staying with me. She had to go back to China, to Lisa and her mother. I held her tight, kissed her and waved goodbye.

I got a cab to a low-key, three-star hotel. Showered and changed into a new tracksuit. Decided to jog the two miles to the gym.

Detroit has been the birthplace to some of the world's toughest fighters, men who clawed their way out of poverty, out of the gutter and the slums. It's part of the history of boxing, turning out a huge number of champions. Places like Kronk not only developed their talent, they also supported communities. That deserves respect. So when I got to the gym, I knocked before I went into the office. Seemed only right.

I placed the Mexican boxing magazine on the desk, right before the eyes of the two old guys seated there. I was on the front page.

"I'm going to be middleweight champion of the world," I said. "Two questions: do you want to make a shit ton of money, and will you help me reach my goal?"

One of the guys, slightly older, looked at me, expressionless. "Why do you think you'll be champ?" he asked. "Because I'm the best there is," I replied. He picked up the magazine, briefly looked at it, glanced at his companion. I saw him nod a yes. The older guy grinned, and said "We've been waiting a long time for you to arrive. You start tomorrow, champ."

We shook hands on the deal, then went over the road to a rundown café. The old guy ordered us the house special. It was surprisingly good. We talked about the fight game. It was in their blood. What they didn't know wasn't worth knowing. Their own gym had suffered in recent years. Hadn't had a champ in a long time. The slightly younger guy, Earl, had been following my Mexican career with some interest. He knew, maybe better than a lot of other trainers would have done, not to dismiss me.

At the end of our meal, I placed $20,000 on the table. "Let's do the place up," I said "A champion should train in style." A week later the builders turned up. Two weeks after that, I passed my medical and got my boxing licence. Two more days, and I was back in the ring. Time for battle.

My opponent was an up-and-coming young guy, hungry for success, carving out his career. I knocked him out and broke his jaw in the first round. Boxing is not for the faint-hearted. I got $3,000. Gave it all to the gym.

That first year out of Detroit, I had fourteen fights and fourteen KOs. I was making a name for myself and slowly moving up the US ranks. It was too easy. Every fight, I switched it on. No fight lasted more than three rounds.

It took 12 months to get where I wanted. The number one contender, in the WBA, WBC and IBF official rankings. The reigning champ had no choice. He had to fight me, or lose his championship belts. His management team didn't make it easy. They weren't stupid, they'd watched me fight. Eventually we signed on the dotted line. We had three months to get ready for the biggest fight of my life.

We flew into Vegas five days beforehand. On the drive to the hotel, billboards along the side of the road showed a familiar faces. Mine, and Marianne's. Marianne Diamond, as she was now. She'd made it. A top slot, in a Vegas nightclub. Funny how life works. We both had top billing in the same crazy town at the same time.

A knock at my door the night before the fight woke me up. I opened my eyes, looked at the clock. It was 10 pm. I needed to sleep. My security guard called out. "You have a visitor."

"At this time?" I snapped. "Who is it?"

"Susan Jones," he said.

Well, now. Interesting. "Let her in," I said, pulling on a robe.

Susan breezed in, sat down and looked at me. "Throw the fight," she said. No preamble, no small talk. Just "Throw the fight."

"I don't think so," I said. "No, I really don't think so. Nice to see you, by the way. How's life?"

I knew exactly how life was. I should so, I'd paid enough to find out. Good job, nice house, husband. Yes. Husband.

I was sitting opposite her. She stood up, put her hand in her bag and pulled out a gun. Pointed it at me. For fuck's sake. Stupid bitch. Couldn't even hold the thing steady. Tears rolled down her face. I ripped my robe open and stepped in close. I held her hands and moved the gun into position, pointing at my chest.

"Shoot me," I said, quietly. "Go ahead. Just do it. I don't give a fuck."

Susan backed off, collapsed on the sofa, sobbing. I'd given her a chance. I moved in fast, yanked the gun out of her hands, pulled her up by her hair and punched her twice in her stomach. I dragged her to the bedroom, pointed the gun at her head. "Undress, bitch," I ordered. "Payback time.

"You set me up with that fucking hooker. You sent me to that fucking hellhole for three years. I helped you, and you repaid me by getting me banged up in prison. Why? For fuck's sake, why?"

She cowered, clutching her clothes to her chest, naked and at my mercy. "Get up," I snarled. "Get onto the bed, face down."

Snivelling, she obeyed. I tied her hands, with the cord from my robe, then fastened it to the top of the bed. I yanked her head towards me, stuffed her panties in her mouth. Reached to the chair beside my bed, drew my belt out of my trousers.

The beating lasted ten long, satisfying minutes. I dropped the belt, sat on the bed, turned her over. Couldn't fuck her. 'Women weaken legs', as the old boxing saying goes. I had willpower. That didn't mean I couldn't have some fun. I stroked her forehead, touched her face, gently kissed her cheek. Put my right hand round her neck and squeezed. At once she was choking, fighting for air, I let go. Bit her neck, then the other side. Stroked and squeezed her breasts and nipples, then bit her left breast hard. My hand moved slowly down her stomach until my fingers reached her box. I prised her legs apart, picked up the gun and pushed it inside her. I pulled the panties out of her mouth.

"Give me one good reason not to pull the fucking trigger," I said. The answer wasn't what I expected.

"You have a son."

"Fuck all to do with me," I said. "I paid for the abortion. Not my problem you didn't have it. Have you told him I'm his dad?"

"Yes," she sobbed. This was a mess. Fuck's sake.

I pulled out the gun. Stuffed the panties back in her mouth, then pushed my hand into her. Two fingers, then three, then my whole fist. I pushed hard. Tears were rolling down her face. "I'm going to kill your husband tomorrow," I said, twisting my hand. "Revenge, you see. You don't fuck with me." I withdrew my hand, and untied her. "Get dressed and fuck off," I said. "I need to rest."

She obeyed, dressed quick. I took her arm, walked her out. I opened the door, looked right and left, shoved her into the hallway and shut the door tight. I went back to the bedroom and closed my eyes, playing the fight out in my mind.

Chapter 31

The following night, I went with my three cornermen into the arena. Caesar's Palace, no less. We went to the changing rooms. I felt super cool. At the pre-fight press conference and weigh in, I'd stared right through him. I'd fucking murder him. Three years in prison, all because of his bitch wife. He was already lost.

A knock at the door. "Five minutes," said a voice. "You ready?" Fuck, yes. I glanced at my cornermen and nodded. We made our way to the ring. I didn't hear the music, didn't hear the crowd. Just the pounding in my own head. I stepped into the ring looked around. There was Ling — no surprise, she'd told me she was coming. Wow, Lisa I wasn't expecting. I raised my gloved hands to them. Marianne was glittering a few rows behind, a fat, rich-looking guy beside her. A huge diamond sparkled on her left hand. That, maybe, explained the sudden rise to fame.

I smiled to myself. My three women, here to witness this highest point in my life. I'd be champ tonight. Marianne smiled and waved. I nodded back. I wondered how she explained me to her husband. I caught Ling's eye. She simply smiled. I was pretty sure she knew about other women in my life.

No time to think about that. An overblown fanfare and some frenetic spotlights announced my opponent. I smiled as he entered the arena, Tina Turner belting out 'Simply the Best'. The fans loved him. What a prick.

I'd done my homework, watched most of his fights. Tonight was going to be a test, for sure. At last, we were both in the centre of the ring, being read the rules. I couldn't tear my eyes away. Finally, the roar of the crowd as the bell went for round one.

Ding. Ding.

He steamed in fast, jab, jab, and back out. Back in, swinging haymakers, trying to knock my head off. I moved faster, powered my fists into his midriff. Backed him up against the ropes. This was fun, a real fight. A real challenge. I unleashed a flurry of blows, head body and arms. He covered up. I stepped back and started to box, bob and weave, jab, jab. This was a twelve-round bout. Not a hope of that.

He was two years my senior. We were both old men, by boxing standards. We were both true champions, both tough nuts to crack. We exchanged blow for blow. It was flat-out entertainment for the crowd. Shaping up to be an epic. Give him his due. He was a good boxer. The bell stopped the first round. Three minutes of the battle was up, and we'd already given the crowd their money's worth.

Round two. I moved in and hit him with a series of sharp, stinging jabs with both fists. One of his eyes started to swell up. His face was red. I switched to his stomach and ribs. Backed him, again, onto the ropes. More jabs to the side of his head. Not too hard, enough to rattle his brain.

He battled back, caught me with a couple of great shots. I hardly felt them. I unleashed a frenzy of punches, careful though, didn't want to knock him out yet. Bang, bang, into his chest, then one more to the side of his head. He wobbled as the bell ended round two.

His cornermen were working fast to patch him up. He'd never been hit so hard. But then, he'd never fought me.

Round three. As the bell sounded, he looked beat, the fight was definitely still on. The hungry crowd roared their approval. I kept hitting the side of his head. It rocked like a baby in a cradle. He grabbed hold, I pushed him back onto the ropes.

A big right hand, then an uppercut, left, right hook. I ducked his wide, swinging punches, went in again to his ribs. He went down on one knee, gasping for breath. A standing eight count from the ref, then back to it. The punches kept coming, head, ribs and kidneys. His arms dropped and a stinging left hook put him down on the canvas again. He was a battler, though. He wanted to hold those titles. He had heart. I knew he'd get up, knew him better than he knew himself. The ref gave him another standing eight count, wiped off his gloves.

He looked at me, nodded, and we went to war again. Round by round, as a hundred million people watched all over the world, I battered my opponent. Give him his due, he gave as good as he got. A great fight. A mighty duel between two legends of the ring. No usual Vegas hype about this fight. Not needed. I let my fists do the talking. I dealt blow after blow. Never too hard, just hard enough to weaken, bit by bit. He was tough, a good boxer. He'd been a tough fighter, a good boxer for too long. He'd taken a lot of punishment. He should have retired. He had the choice. Sadly, like many older boxers, he thought he had one more good fight in him. They don't know when to stop. I did. I'd retire tonight, right after this fight.

Toe-to-toe, we exchanged hooks, jabs, uppercuts, haymakers. We grappled, bounced each other off the ropes. The bell rang, again and again. By the time we reached the end of Round Five, his cornermen had no hope of patching him up. His belts were slipping out of his grasp, and there was nothing he could do. Time to finish it.

I glanced over towards Susan and my opponent's entourage. She knew the score. I'd told her what would happen, and she knew it was coming. Never mind, she'd look good in black.

The big money was on me, for a 6th round knockout. I'd predicted it in the press. What a laugh. None of my fights had ever gone six rounds. I'd had a hard time making sure this one did. His cornermen were trying to throw in the towel. He was a brave man, wouldn't let them. One of his eyes was swollen almost shut. His mouth hung open. His muscles were quivering with fatigue. Ding, ding. Round 6.

Before I signed the contract, I stipulated the fight had to be on 6th June. The sixth day of the sixth month. And I'd stop the fight in the sixth round. My numbers, you see. 666. I went in for the kill. He didn't stand a chance. I let lose a frenzy of jaw-breakers, left jab, right hook, uppercuts, and followed with a volley to his sore and most likely already cracked ribs. I backed him against the ropes, one last time. The world stood still as I drew back for the hardest right hand I'd ever thrown. I watched it connect in slow motion. As he started his fall, I smashed a huge left uppercut to his unguarded chin and big right hand, to his nose. One final blow, with all my power, right in front of his heart. I'd never hit anyone that hard.

I actually felt pain for the first time that night. I was human after all.

Face down, he lay motionless. His cornermen rushed into the ring. A doctor got in, too late. The crowd was eerily silent. Nonetheless, I raised my arms in victory. I was middleweight champion of the world.

•

Chapter 32

See, here's the thing. If he'd just agreed to meet me, all those years before, it might have been different. If he'd allowed Lisa and me into his life, accepted his family, he'd still have been champion, still have been alive. Might still have been married to Susan. Since she'd fucked me over, her time was coming too.

The description the whore Julie had given took me back to Susan. One of the calls I made was to my private investigator. What he discovered was almost funny. She was married to my brother. Of all the fucking people she could have met at uni, she met him. And married him. Married, had a kid. Although, it turns out, the kid was mine.

Apparently, the blood in my grandfather's veins ran strong in my brother and me. Like me, he'd taken up boxing at an early age. Unlike me, he didn't carry all the venom and rage caused by our abandonment. He'd never killed anyone in the ring, accidentally or otherwise. He'd been a clean fighter, a good sportsman, and had earned his titles fairly and with honour.

Fucker.

Well. He'd been given a choice. He'd chosen to turn his back. I fucking hated him for that. I wanted him to suffer, to feel my pain. To die. Now Susan would suffer, too. Maybe even die. I'd bide my time.

I went back to the changing room. My guys were silent as they cut the tape off my gloves, then the knuckle bandages. My trainer looked at my right hand. "It's broken," he said. I looked at the two swollen knuckles. He was probably right. I didn't give a fuck, it would heal. I showered, walked back. The room was empty. The guys had disappeared. Why? We always went for steak, after a fight. Maybe they were tired. Fuck it, I was tired too.

I dried off, trunks on. Felt weary, sat down. Reached into my bag and pulled out my book. Then the door burst open. I stood up, just as a guy charged in, shouting. He had a knife in his right hand. He stabbed me. I didn't even try to stop him. I was too tired. I just fell to the floor, my book flying from my hands. I stared at my stomach as blood oozed from my wounds. I gazed up. Was I dreaming? They were all there. Ling, Lisa, Susan and Marianne. All staring at me. I tried to retrieve my book. Fell back on the concrete floor instead.

I woke. My eyes were sore, the light was too bright. Then I went out again. Next thing I remember was waking, in a quiet room. Lisa and Ling were by my bed. I cast an eye over them, their red eyes showed they'd been crying. I tried to raise my arms, to comfort them. Lisa held my right hand, Ling held my left. I couldn't lift them. My strength had gone. I coughed. "I won," I said. "I won the fight."

Ling touched my forehead. "Where am I?" I asked.

"Hospital, my husband," said Ling.

A flash of memory. "My book," I asked. "Where's my book?"

"It's by your side," she said, pointing to the bedside cabinet.

A nurse and doctor appeared to check me over. Ling held a half-full cup of water to my lips. I felt calm and relaxed, I was almost floating. I smiled at my beautiful wife. "I'm here," she said. "I'll take care of you."

The days and nights passed slowly. My injuries had been a lot worse than I'd thought. I'd lost a lot of blood in the attack. Four weeks later, I was out, with all-clear to travel. Ling had, as always, arranged everything. I was wheeled out of the hospital to a waiting ambulance, taken to the airport and loaded on the private jet. On my way, once again, to China. Ling took me to the cabin. Time to rest and recover. Ling knew I needed time on my own. She stayed at the house with her mum. Came to see me every day. Stayed some nights. I had my book with me.

Another cabin had been built on the mountain, larger, fitted with all mod cons. I walked a little each day. As the weeks turned into months, my strength returned. My bodyguards kept a watchful eye out. Lisa visited often. A woman therapist came to see me every day. I talked with her about different subjects, mostly about Ling.

Her loyalty and devotion meant a great deal to me. I spoke about Lisa and my family. She asked me about the attack. I said exactly what I would have said to the police, although they never interviewed me. They had plenty of eyewitnesses and the guy was locked up, awaiting trial.

Eventually, we finished a course of therapy. The next day would be her last visit. She wanted Ling and Lisa present. I shrugged. Fine by me.

"We want you to watch this," the therapist said, Ling and Lisa seated on either side. She pressed a button on her laptop. The video didn't last long, less than a minute. Grainy security footage from the changing rooms. It started with me, sitting on the bench. I reached into my bag and got out my book. The door burst open, the guy with the knife burst in. I just stood there while he stabbed me. As I fell to the floor, my stomach covered in blood, Ling, Marianne, Lisa, and Susan ran into the room. I'd dropped my book and was staring at my wounds. The guy was kneeling down, still stabbing me. I was just trying to retrieve my book. I didn't try to defend myself.

Ling reacted the quickest and disarmed my attacker with ease. Two security guards came in, handcuffed the guy and took him away. I tried to sit up, then fell back, covered in blood. The faces of the onlookers showed total horror. Ling was trying to stop the bleeding with towels. The footage stopped.

"Why did you show me this?" I asked.

"You needed to see what happened," she replied.

Fucking hell, I thought. I already knew what happened. I was there.

"Why didn't you defend yourself?" said Ling.

Tough question. I had to be honest. You reap what you sow, although farming was not one of my strong points. "He was my son," I answered. "How could I hurt him?"

I knew why he'd stabbed me. He fucking hated me. Just like I hated my dad. My missing, cowardly, piece-of-shit dad. And then I'd killed the man who'd tried his best to take the place I should have filled. My only brother.

I looked at my wife. "Susan was pregnant before she moved to the States," I said. "I thought she'd had an abortion. I gave her the cash for it, made the appointment… she didn't do it. The boy who stabbed me was my son."

Chapter 33

Acouple of hours later, the therapist gone, I sat with my wife and my sister, eating a light lunch on the patio. Ling reached over and touched my hand. "I have a special surprise for you," she said, getting up. "Please, don't be angry."

Angry? Why would I be angry? I didn't say anything. Ling left us. Half an hour later, she was back, holding a little girl's hand.

"Say hello to your father, Mei Ying," she said. I was speechless. This beautiful little thing was my daughter. Already five years old. A little bit shy, nervous of this strange, scarred man. I smiled down. "Hello," I said. "How are you? I'm very pleased to meet you."

Now I knew why Ling had looked so different when I'd seen her at the prison. She was a mum. I didn't ask why she hadn't told me. No need to ask. It didn't matter. I had a daughter. A beautiful, sweet, trusting child. This was what life was about. Only this. Family.

As the quiet weeks passed, Ling and Mei Ying visited me every day. Her name meant Beautiful Flower. I thought it was perfect. She spoke Chinese and English, had been home-schooled by top teachers. We walked and talked endlessly, Mei holding my hand like she never wanted to let go. Ling was always close by, our constant shadow.

The weeks turned into months. Mei was dazzling, a brilliant ray of sunshine, my wonderful girl. I spoke to Ling about the business. We'd lost the lot when I was in prison. She'd fought hard, another Triad gang had seized control. She had no choice, in the end, but to flee. We were safe in China, we had a hell of a lot of enemies out there.

Ling sighed. "Let's just live our lives, James," she said. "We have more than enough money, more than we'll ever spend. We have a beautiful child, a good life here. Why chase trouble? We've had enough to last a lifetime, and more."

It was decided. I'd move into the main house, at Christmas. Focus on my family. Live the life I'd always dreamed of. No drama. No stress. No voices screaming in my head. One thing still played on my mind.

Christmas Eve. They were all waiting to welcome me. I looked around the room. It was wonderful. Ling, her mum, my daughter, my sister Lisa. And, a surprise guest of honour: Marianne. They'd bonded, back in Vegas, over my broken body. A mutual understanding had been reached. Rather than fight over me, they'd share. Chinese tradition allows for more than one wife, after all. Something in Ling's cultural background remembered that, and honoured it.

There were Christmas decorations everywhere. A huge tree, dazzling with lights and tinsel, a mound of presents underneath. A log fire sparked and crackled, filling the room with warmth and the smell of burning wood. Background music filtered through the noise of greeting.

"Everything okay, my husband?" asked Ling, taking my hand. "Yes," I said. "Thank you. Thank you for making this happen." I kissed her, then swung my little daughter into my arms and danced her around to the cheesy Christmas songs.

Lisa smiled and joined us, she loved to dance. Marianne sang along, her beautiful voice making even those jaded old tunes sound great. I raised my glass of mineral water and thanked her for coming. Everything was more than good. Everything was wonderful. I was home.

It was late, well past Mei's bedtime, so Ling went to tuck her in and go to bed herself. The others followed suit, we'd be up early the next day, with an excited five-year-old to entertain. I couldn't wait for my first Christmas with my daughter. To recover from some of the excitement, I walked into the frosted garden. The moon was high and clear. I shadow boxed for half an hour, then press ups, sit ups, low front kicks, high front kicks. I practiced elbow and knee strikes, palm strikes, then the Dim Mak. I stretched for 20 minutes, warm despite the freezing temperature. Then I showered, went to bed and slept soundly, my arm around my wife.

Christmas day with Mei. A magical time. I felt great. Hugged my wonderful wife, my wonderful sister, my wonderful child. Even hugged Marianne, which felt strange. Part of me was still wondering why she'd agreed to come. I knew she and Ling had reached a strange kind of friendship, it still didn't make much sense. After a traditional Western turkey lunch, with all the trimmings, I ushered her into the courtyard. "It's great to see you," I said. "It really is. But—"

"You don't understand why I've come," she said. I nodded. "I came to warn you," she said. "Because… because I love you. Please listen,' she went on, as I opened my mouth to interrupt.

Marianne was married to a Russian billionaire. I'd seen her with him, at the fight. Heard stories about him later on. He was a powerful man, ex KGB. Heavily involved, the stories said, in weapons dealing in African countries. Probably Russian mafia. She'd heard him talk to his associates. This was the point where I fetched Ling.

"We must protect ourselves," he'd said. "We must eliminate all threats. Kill this 'Candy Man'," he'd said. Marianne knew I owned the Candy Man shops. She'd made the connection. She'd given me the advantage. I'd been warned.

The Russian was in his homeland, dealing with urgent business. She was flying back to France tonight, aboard our jet. "Thank you," I said, on our way to the airport. "You didn't have to do this. It was brave of you."

Her parting words were: "Yes I did, James. I'm in love with you."

Bit of a mindfuck, to be honest. I hadn't given her much reason to. I had a family to protect, back at the house. I found Ling and Lisa playing board games with Mei. I looked at Ling. "I need my stuff, please," I said. She took me upstairs.

Laid out neatly on the bed were all the weapons I'd need. Two new handguns, a compact submachine gun, plenty of ammo and a long-range sniper rifle. My katana and two new flick knives with solid silver handles engraved with a dragon. They were magnificent. I thanked my wife. She was, as always, the best. I'd be ready, if or when they came.

I told Ling my plan. She was hesitant. It seemed dangerous. In my crazy mind, it was the only way. Let them come. This was my battle.

I was the Candy Man.

Two days later, I waved my family off on the jet, off to a safe destination, far away from me. I sent all the staff and guards to a hotel in town with envelopes of cash. Keep them all out of the way. I sat in the lounge, drank a coffee, made an important phone call. Picked up my fully-stocked rucksack. Leaving a note on the kitchen table, I went out the back door, closed it behind me and started walking.

— • —

Chapter 34

The cold wind took my breath. Winter was not a time for the faint -hearted. It was like mountain conditioning in the Legion all over again. Eventually, I reached the cabin, lit a fire, drank some hot soup. I'd make my stand here on the mountain.

I left the oil lanterns burning and left the cabin, positioned myself higher up, with an excellent vantage point of the steep slopes below. Just one narrow, rocky, icy path, from the valley to the cabin. I didn't know the number of men they'd send.

On the third night, slowly making their way up the path, came 30 men, all armed to the teeth. The snow had been falling heavily all day. Despite that, they moved with military precision. I watched through the telescopic sights as they circled the cabin, smiled as the guy in charge did his hand signals. Eight men went inside. I'd made a dummy in the bed, to look like someone was sleeping there. The bedroom was in darkness. I heard shots, then pressed the remote detonator I held in my hand. The explosion set off a chain reaction like something out of the Bible. Nature took over.

An avalanche brutally destroys anything in its way. Millions of tons of snow came hurtling down the mountain, huge boulders bounding through it all. I moved back into my small cave and hoped I'd find a way out. They were all buried by the snow and ice. The cabin would have to be rebuilt again. Damn. I had fond memories of that place.

I put my thermal hat on, an extra warm winter coat, got in my sleeping bag and opened my book. My family was safe. That's all that mattered. I dozed off, buried in the cave.

I knew the Candy Man would have to return, to seek retribution. That's why I'd made the call, left the note at the house. It took them five days to find me. It was a close call. The Grand Master and his monks dug me out, shivering and starving. I went with them to their ancient Shaolin temple. Shaved my head, donned a grey uniform, did the daily chores, meditated. Just like them.

I trained for hours each day, honing my skills harder than I'd ever done before. I drew strength from the mountains, toned my body and mind. It was a simple life. I spent a lot of time with the Grand Master. I listened to his wise words, studied Buddhism. I only stayed for three months. I wasn't put on this planet to be a monk. No way.

We parted company. I packed my small rucksack, said my goodbyes. Thanked them all, especially the Grand Master. They'd saved me in more ways than one. I left a bag full of US dollars to help with the upkeep of the magnificent temple I'd been privileged to call home and started my pilgrimage towards my true destiny.

It was going to be a long journey. You take the first step, then keep going.

I walked for ten days, until I reached the Great Wall in Jiayuguan, Gansu. Spectacular. What a feat, to build something like that, so long ago. Inspiring. If that was possible, anything was. I missed my wife and family, spoke to them in my head every day. I felt they were with me on my journey.

In Jiayuguan, having made a bit of space between me and my enemies, who would surely expect me to take a more direct route, I bought a clapped out old car at a ridiculous price, and drove for two days to Xi'an, home of the terracotta warriors. I'd bring Mei to see them one day. No time now. I found a small hotel, showered, shaved, fully cleansed for the first time in almost two weeks. Next day, I boarded the train to Beijing.

Two days later, smartly dressed, I walked in to an oh-so-familiar Chinese restaurant. I walked up to a table filled with smoking Chinese playing cards. "You owe me money," I said, dropping a bag of candy on the table. "I've come to collect."

These were the Triads who had stolen our business. Eight shops, 44 franchised shops, two clubs and a casino. We hadn't seen a penny of income in over five years. That was a lot of money. About twenty-five million, by my maths. And that was being cautious. There was a recession on, after all.

The card game froze as I dropped my calling card on the table. They looked at it, then back at me. I had their full attention. At the well-trained men, standing behind me. Four drew their weapons, pointed the guns at me. I drew out my phone, handed it to the boss. "Watch this," I said. "You best sit down," I told the men.

It was a short video of his wife and his two sons. Tied. Terrified. I'd done my homework. Again I said, as I took my phone out of his sweaty hand, "You owe me money."

He ordered his men to lower their weapons. Staring at me with fear in his eyes, he asked, "How much?"

"Twenty-five million should save your family," I said. "Tell your men to drop their weapons into this bag."

I put a bag on the table. Six more of my men entered the restaurant with submachine guns, balaclavas over their heads. "You don't know who you're dealing with," said the boss. I laughed. Well, it was a fucking daft thing to say. "Sure I do," I answered. "You're the guys who stole our business and our money.

"See, I have a reputation to protect," I went on. "This is about honour. This is about my wife's honour. My wife: Ling Wang."

Ah. Now he knew the score. We tied them all up, hands behind their backs, except him. "Open the safe," I told him. He did as I ordered. I put the cash in a black holdall. Maybe a couple of hundred grand. A drop in the ocean. Then we opened a laptop next to him. My guy sat down, ready. "Your bank information, please," I said. He hesitated. I screwed the silencer on my gun, looked at the snaked tattooed on his neck and shot him through his right leg. "Isn't your family worth twenty-five million?" I asked. He gulped, reeled off the information we needed.

I gave my guy a piece of paper with my account details on. I turned the computer away from prying eyes as I entered my password. We transferred the required amount to my account. Still fifteen million in his. I'd been far too conservative.

"Might as well transfer the rest," I said. "He won't need it."

Business proceedings complete, I nodded to him. "Thanks for looking after our business," I said. No substitute for good manners. I gave the nod to one of my men. He went out, then came back in with the boss's wife and teenage sons, still tied and gagged. They were pushed to their knees in front of me.

"Leave no loose ends," I said, as I squeezed the trigger. Wife first, then sons. One bullet each. I turned the gun on him. "You fucked with the Candy Man," I said, simply, as he joined his family. I'd learned a valuable lesson back in Vegas, with Susan and my teenage son. No loose ends, ever again.

We marched the rest of his gang out to the waiting van, got them in, shot them all. The van would be dumped later. I went back into the restaurant and sat down. A mug of coffee appeared. It was the happy old manager, glad to see his place back in the right hands.

I checked my phone. The two clubs and our casino were back in our hands. The rest of the Snake gang would disperse, leaderless. They knew what they were up against now. It was a good night's work.

We drove to the flat, where I opened the door for the first time in years. It looked the same, apart from the dust. My men hauled all the bags of cash upstairs to the lounge. Fuck it, I'd buy a money counting machine. I wasn't going through all this. I had new managers and staff in place at the clubs and casino. We were back in business.

Next morning, I waited outside my shop. I let two Chinese women in. They'd start making the amazing fudge again that day. Two guys would act as security at each shop. New managers would open the rest today. Delivery vans and motorbikes were ready. I had over 100 men working for me, all dragon Triads. Time to focus on my next task.

Late evening, a week later, six of my men with me, we parked 100 yards from my target. He was a creature of habit. At 10 pm, he'd exit his restaurant, then go to the brothel he owned. Timing was of the utmost importance. My phone buzzed. Ling, confirming that the big boss in Moscow had been murdered by an unknown assassin. Decapitated with a sword. A bag of candy lay by his headless body.

Ling was an amazing woman.

I put my phone on the dashboard, got out of the Merc, took off my long winter coat and walked into the shadows, drawing my weapons, ready for the kill. Four bodyguards came out first. A driver sat waiting, engine running. Same as the previous seven nights. I closed my eyes, playing out the forthcoming events in my mind. Sure enough, the Russian came out, right on time. I raised two specially-made 14-inch swords and charged in before anyone had a chance to get to draw weapons. The waiting car was rammed by a van at the same time as the driver was shot by one of my men. Five Russians, dead. It was all so easy.

I wiped the blood off my swords on the dead guy's coat, and put them safely back in their leather sheaths. I dropped the obligatory bag of candy on the blood-soaked pavement, stepped over the bodies, walked to the Merc, and drove back to Chinatown. The next day, the Candy Man killings made only the inside pages of the tabloids. The front pages were global breaking news. A hot, hot story. A Russian billionaire, dead, his private jet blown up on take-off. Survived by his beautiful wife, international singing star Marianne Diamond.

Marianne was free. She could live her dream. Another debt paid.

I went up to the flat above the shop, missing my wife, my child. I made coffee, went to the lounge and sat down. I looked at my reflection in the window. I smiled. I was back. I was the Candy Man.

———————————————— • ————————————————

Chapter 35

Business was brisk. Our five brothels now reopened. New managers at both our clubs and the casino. I'd increased everyone's pay by 20%. Only fair for them to share in our success. I was a good boss, a good guy. Time to reunite with my family. I was only a short plane ride away if there was any trouble. I didn't expect any.

I phoned my wife, spoke to Mei, and headed off to Monte Carlo. As I jumped on the yacht, I was greeted with a smile and a "Bonjour, Papa!" Mei was learning French words. I hugged my beautiful little girl. My breath of fresh air. I gave her a gift, turned to her mother. She leaped into my arms, a special moment. I'd missed them both so much. This was the life.

I gazed out over the harbour as Ling took Mei to bed. They'd had a long journey. I read Mei a short story, said goodnight, wished her sweet dreams. Then Ling and I went out on the town, leaving her in the care of her nanny and six heavily-armed, more-than-capable bodyguards. A meal, conversation. There was a lot to catch up on.

Back at the boat, back to our room. Time for some more catching up. We spent the night getting reacquainted, calmly, passionately, slowly. I spent two glorious weeks like that, with my family. Walks, shopping. I bought Ling and Mei anything they wanted. On our last night in Monte Carlo, Ling and I talked.

She was going back to China. I understood why. It was her home, the place she loved. I was tempted to go back too, but our business needed my leadership. Fear is the key factor. Fear of the Candy Man. Next day, I watched as they boarded the jet, waved them off. I'd work out a way to be with them.

One more week in France. It was time to visit an old friend. I decided to take to the open road. Not the Merc. Instead I strapped a small rucksack tight across my shoulders and swung onto a brand new Ducati Sport 1000. Long time since I'd ridden a motorbike. This was going to be fun. Just under three exhilarating hours later, I arrived in Marseille. Lying on my king-size bed in a five-star hotel, I dialled a number.

"Bonjour, James," she said. I had a hard-on, just hearing her voice. "Hello Marianne," I said. "How are you?"

I told her where I was staying. She said she'd be there in 30 minutes. I lay on the bed, shut my eyes and waited, picturing the fun time to come.

She looked stunning. As she leaned in to kiss me, lust shrivelled and died. Half pissed, she stank of booze. "Have you eaten tonight?" I asked. "No," she said, shaking her head in exaggerated movements. I took her hand, led her down to the restaurant. Her careful walk gave away the fact that she was even drunker than I'd thought.

I was frustrated, angry. I wanted to play with this luscious body, beat her senseless and then fuck her like a whore. Just like old times. But this wasn't arousing in the least. Maybe I'd changed, grown up. Ling was a loyal, devoted wife. She loved me. I had, eventually, grown to love her. And I'd die to protect her and Mei.

I was in lust with Marianne, not love. And that lust hadn't survived her drunken, slurring, stinking state. There'd been too much of that in my younger days for it to be appealing. So instead we ate, talked about her plans, what she wanted to do, now she was a widow. She drank most of a bottle of wine while I sipped a mineral water. Meal over, she wanted to go back to my room. Instead, I took her to the main entrance, asked the doorman to hail a cab. I held her arm, sat with her in the lobby.

"Don't waste your life, Marianne," I said, gently. "It's too precious. You have talent, you have looks. You have a good heart. Do something good with it all." I kissed her cheek, led her to the waiting cab. Shut the door, turned and walked out of her life.

I went to my hotel room and phoned Ling. I must have woken her. "James?" she said. "Are you okay?"

"I'm fine, Ling," I said. "In fact, I'm good. I just wanted to tell you something. I love you."

The first time I'd said those words in all these years. Suddenly,

I knew what I wanted. To be with Ling and Mei. "See you soon," I said, and hung up.

I booked a flight online, packed my bag. I'd surprise her when I got to China. Rode the motorbike to Paris, dumped it at the airport. A stop in London first to brief my team.

My right-hand man was waiting when I walked into the restaurant. I knew I could trust him. He'd been one of the monks I'd trained with, back in China. He left the contemplative life, married. His wife was chief housekeeper at Ling's family home in China, living there with their two sons. He knew if he crossed me, they'd all die. Keep things simple.

I told him my plan. Keep the expansion going, keep stamping down hard on enemy action. Here are the people you need to pay off. Here are the officials you need to bribe. Here are the people we know to be loyal. Here are the ones to watch. I wanted weekly reports on every aspect of the business, monthly oversight of the books. Otherwise, he had my full approval to step into my shoes. To become the Candy Man in my absence.

Then I called Ling, to tell her I was coming home.

Chapter 36

Four days later, I boarded our jet. I was going to be with my family. I felt calm and relaxed as we touched down in Hami. I was fast-tracked through customs with my hand luggage, all I had with me. My family was there to greet me. Ling and Mei, smiling from ear to ear. I'd see my sister soon. I'd realized that home is not a building, not a country. Home is where your loved ones are. I was home.

We got in the waiting Merc and drove to the house. Our driver, one bodyguard, both trained and armed. Two cars in front, two cars behind, both with heavily-armed guards ready to protect my family. I relaxed, chatted with my daughter. By the time we reached the house, I was weary. I went up to my room, lay down. Ling slipped in beside me, stroking my forehead. "Rest now, my husband," she said. "Rest."

Tired as I was, rest wouldn't come. I stared into the darkness. Ling's breathing slowed as she fell asleep. I got up without disturbing her, covered her beautiful body. Quietly, I sat down by the window and gazed up to the stars. I was still there when dawn broke. A magnificent sunrise.

Ling woke. She smiled as the cover slipped from her naked body. I got up, removed my clothes and joined her. We made love as the sunlight cascaded into our room. Warm, familiar, comforting, somehow also a new beginning.

Mei was waiting for us downstairs. We had breakfast together, as a family should. I spent the day with them, walking in the large gardens. Early summertime, plants blossomed everywhere. Birds sang in the branches, crickets chirped. Blue sky above, a broad, free landscape all around. Nature at its best. We played games with Mei. She was learning Tai Chi, showed me her moves. A wonderful day.

That night, after dinner, Ling handed me a folder. She didn't say a word. I opened it, stared at the photo inside. Felt a wave of emotion sweep over me. Shock. Triumph. Rage. Most of all, rage. The private eye had found my dad. Lisa's dad. Now the prick was going to fucking die.

A week later, I was on my way up the mountain path to the Shaolin temple. I needed to see Grand Master. I banged on the old oak gates, it wasn't the Master who opened them. It was my old AC from the French Foreign Legion. I swallowed my anger, kept a poker face.

He smiled. "Welcome," he said. "We've been waiting for you. Come on in."

As I entered, the AC shut and locked the gate behind me. I bowed to the Master. "Why have you come?" he asked. "To find inner peace," I replied.

"You will not find it here," he said. I nodded. This was a signal. They'd all known I was going to come.

I stood in the centre of the old courtyard and looked around. So much time spent here, so much training. Ling and I had been the master's star pupils. He'd taught us everything he knew. The monks were well trained, only to a point. The rest was known only to Grand Master, and us two.

The monks stood silent, watching. I turned to the AC. "Why have you come here?" I asked.

"To kill you," he said. Matter of fact. No drama. You had to admire the man.

He held a sword in his right hand. The Master smiled as he passed his own sword to me. He knew the score.

"Now we fight," said the AC.

"Are you fucking mad?" I said, smiling. "You've seen what happens when people fight me."

He shrugged, and gave a shrill whistle. Twenty guys appeared, all armed with sub-machine guns aimed towards the monks. All Chinese. Six others slid out of hiding. I recognised other former colleagues from the Legion.

"You fight," he said. "Fight, or the monks all die." I shook my head, sadly. "It's nothing personal," he added. "Just another well-paid job."

He'd told me he was going to be a mercenary. Looked like he was doing well as one. "Who's your paymaster?" I asked, swinging the sword, warming up. He laughed. "Your wife," he said.

I stood absolutely still.

"You think she doesn't know about you? About the whores?" he sneered. "You think she doesn't know that if you live here, she loses everything? Her pride, her dignity, her power? Face it, son. You're a cold-blooded killer. You chose this life. You chose this end."

I burst out laughing. He blinked.

"You made a huge mistake, coming here," I said. He smiled, shook his head. Cocky old bastard. "Open your eyes," I said. "Look around."

I pulled aside my collar, revealing the dragon on my neck. At that moment, all the Chinese gunmen, all the monks, did the same. I nodded. The gunmen turned their weapons, pointed them at the AC and the ex-legionnaires.

I turned to them. "Drop your weapons," I said. They did. They were tied up, hands behind their backs, forced to kneel. Only the AC was left standing. I took his gun from his hip holster, checked it was loaded, turned and shot my former comrades. One shot each. No time to fuck about.

I glared at the AC. "Now's your chance," I said. "Earn your pay."

This temple, unknown to him, held a secret. It may have begun as a Shaolin retreat, today it was our training camp. Ling's late father had set it up. New initiates and young family members came to learn new and deadly fighting skills. The population of 'monks' changed all the time, as recruits came, trained, graduated and moved on. The AC had been brought into a trap.

My wife had played a blinder.

I moved to my fighting stance. The Major raised his sword, ready to strike. This was going to be fun. I smiled. I'd waited a long time for this moment.

We moved slow, stalking each other, swords ready. He lunged at me, I moved out of the way. Our blades clashed. He was pretty quick for an old guy. He lunged again. I jumped and spun, thrusting out my blade, catching his lower leg behind his unguarded knee. He thrust again, desperately, as his leg gave way. I struck again, a downward blow that severed his sword hand at the wrist. Blood spurted from the wound. He was kneeling before me. The battle was almost over. For the first time in my life, I felt tears run down my face.

Chapter 37

"You dare call me son?" I gasped out, collapsing to my knees in front of him. "You? You have no right! You left us! Left me as a baby! Left my mum! She died. We needed you! A newborn baby and two young kids, and you fucking ran away, abandoned us! Why the fuck would you do that? Why? Why? You're a fucking coward, a fucking thief, you stole my life!"

I stared into his eyes. He stared back, eyes wide. Fearful. "Yes," I went on. "I'm a cold-blooded killer. And you made me what I am. Hating you, every day, my whole life. I am who I am because of you. All because of you."

I held out a hand. One of the monks handed me my bag. I reached in, pulled out book, the book I'd carried with me my whole life. I laid it on the ground in front of him. The pages blew open in the breeze. He stared at it, at the wedding photos I'd glued in. My mum and him. They looked so happy.

A photo of my mum, proudly wearing her karate uniform, a black belt tied around her waist. She was so beautiful. An old newspaper cutting, mum and him outside their shop. A sweet shop. The sign overhead: The Candy Man. Handmade chocolates and fudge. The business collapsed after she died. My grandpa, holding his boxing belt. Another, in his French Foreign Legion uniform, white cap blazing. My whole life, mapped out on these pages.

And him, in front of me. The source of it all. All the anger, hatred, the need for revenge. He was to blame, for everything. All the deaths. All the violence. All because he fucking ran away and left us for dead. Like we were nothing.

I hadn't recognised him when I'd joined the Legion. He was 20 years old in the photo. He looked different with a beard. He'd spoken French, his accent flawless to my untrained ear. If I'd known him, he'd have died then. A slow, painful death. Now I knew him. Now he'd die.

He was mumbling, incoherent. Didn't matter. There was nothing he could have said. And I wasn't listening anyway. It was all too late.

The last page of the book flipped open. My drawing.

Now he knew what was coming. He saw it on the page. I'd added to it over the years. Him kneeling, hand cut off, knives in his eyes, no ears. A sword through his chest. Flames, flames all around.

He looked up at me.

His ears first, two precision moves with the sword. I counted to ten, then drew my two flick-knives, clicked them open, thrust them in his eyes. Drew back my sword, paused to savour the moment. Rammed it, with all my strength, right through his stone-cold stone heart. I looked at him lying there, broken. Spat in his face. Fucking coward. "Burn in hell, old man," I said.

I stood, picked up my book. Brushed off some dust. Took a deep breath. Job complete.

I closed the book and put it back in my rucksack. I looked over to the Grand Master. He hadn't moved. No-one had. "Time for some herbal tea, I think," I said.

———————————— ● ————————————

Chapter 38

While the monks cleaned up the mess, I went with the Master to his private courtyard. A servant brought us tea.

"We need to up the training," I said. "We need more men, and fast." Our business was expanding, going international. First, Candy Man shops in New York. Then Vegas and Miami. Then France, and the rest of Europe. We were branching into weapons, had new contracts in the pipeline. Lisa was working on them. Ling was overseeing the new factory, here in the local town. We'd create employment, wealth. A successful, self-contained economy for the people living around us. That would keep us safe.

I'd run it all from China. I was going to be a full-time dad.

I finished my tea, shook hands with the Master and slowly walked back down the rocky path. My convoy of three cars was waiting for me at the end of the path.

We pulled into the long sweeping driveway through the large landscaped garden, up to the four stone steps leading to my oak front door. I got out, went in, footsteps echoing on the Italian marble floor. The huge crystal chandelier came to life, as I switched on the lights. "I'm home," I called.

My beautiful daughter came running down the grand spiral stairs to greet me. I smiled and hugged her. Then my wife walked in. "Hello James," she said. "How was your day? Supper will be ready soon."

This was my home. A happy home, filled with love and laughter. With family. I was living my dream.

Lisa also came in and greeted me with a hug. "Don't worry," I whispered. "Ling's not cooking tonight. The chefs are on duty." I could hear her laughing as I made way up the stairs.

I showered, dressed in the clothes Ling had laid out for me. White shirt, black suit, red tie, polished black brogues. We sat together, enjoyed a family meal. When we'd done, Ling stood up, walked around the table to me. She handed me an old wooden box. I opened it. The gold chain and medallion. I was officially the boss. I'd reached my goal. Top of the heap. The world's most successful businessman.

One day, Ling, Lisa and I would rule the world. We'd rain death and destruction on anyone who got in the way. This wasn't the end. It was a new beginning. I guess I should have thanked my dad. He helped get me there. It was all because of him.

The Candy Man was going global. A dark storm was on its way.